PRAISE FOR THE
EXPONENTIAL APOCALYPSE
SERIES

"[*Exponential Apocalypse*] definitely owes some inspiration to Douglas Adams, albeit with more 'f-bombs' and hookers than I recall seeing in the *Hitchhiker's Guide*."

– Jason Dorough, Fandomania

"If *The Avengers* was written by Terry Pratchett and directed by Kevin Smith, you might end up in the same dimension as *Dead Presidents*. Eirik Gumeny's sequel to *Exponential Apocalypse* is a weird, wild ride through post-post-apocalyptic America. And it's dead funny."

– Kat Clay, Radiant Attack

"I'll take this Thor over any of the Marvel Thors any day."

– Stephen Schwegler, author of *Perhaps*. and *Gag*

"This should be the next show on Adult Swim."

– lady on Amazon.com

ALSO BY THE AUTHOR

an *Exponential Apocalypse* novella
by Eirik Gumeny

Jersey Devil Press
www.jerseydevilpress.com

BLACK HOLE, SON!

Jersey Devil Press
Red Bank, NJ

www.jerseydevilpress.com

1st Edition

ISBN 978-0-9859062-8-3

For Monica

"All good things must come to an end. Preferably in a humongous explosion."

– "Into the Wild Green Yonder," *Futurama*

BLACK HOLE, SON!

PREVIOUSLY,
ON EXPONENTIAL APOCALYPSE

"THERE HAVE BEEN," BEGINS A DARK, HEAVY VOICE, "TWENTY-seven-and-a-half apocalypses to date."

A montage of news clips and shaky cell phone footage flashes across the screen: meteorites slamming into a strip mall; the flaming wreckage of a massive alien warship crashing into Times Square; Santa's Workshop exploding; zombies; more zombies; a robot ripping the spine out of a human resistance fighter.

"The Earth," continues the voice, "has been moved ... and razed ... and rebuilt ..."

More stock footage: enormous particle colliders spooling up in the Antarctic wilderness; the chrome-and-carbon steel skyline of the Kingdom of Los Alamos shimmering in the sunlight; the Empire State Building sinking into dark, sludgy waters.

"... a couple of times."

The scientist-kings of Los Alamos, bank boxes in hands, being forced from their offices at gunpoint; seething hordes of turkeys; massive mechanical cranes and literal boatloads of trash, arriving for the rebuilding of New New York.

"And while there is no known correlation between calamities," continues the voice, "a surprising number of these Armageddons seem to have either been caused, or *kind of* caused, and sometimes stopped ..."

A half-naked British Indian woman and a completely naked clone of the sexy version of Chris Pratt punch wave after wave of old ladies in the face. The camera pulls back, revealing a shirtless, caped Australian man holding a cartoonishly large three-pronged plug in one hand and a matching orange extension cord in the other. With terrific fanfare, he puts them together.

"... by the men and woman who would come to be known as the Vegas Four, the heroes of the Las Vegas Massacre."

A series of ornately-produced shots in quick succession: The Australian man, bare chest glistening, pulls a glowing hammer from his thick belt and points it at an enormous dragon-monster. The British Indian woman, in a short skirt and tight leather corset, pulls a coruscating half-sword from her back and points it a megalomaniacal underwear model. A clone of the fat, stoner version of Chris Pratt punches a frothing cow in the face repeatedly. An enormous blob of a man, folds of fat on top of folds of other fat, sits in an ornate bathtub in an almost infinite field of skulls, laughing maniacally.

Then: An unnecessarily handsome man appears on-screen, walking slowly in front of a dark red curtain.

"Join us," he says, "as we hear from Thor Oddinson, the former Scandinavian Lord of Thunder; Queen Victoria the Xth, warrior princess; Jesús Herschel Christ, the –" A pair of exaggerated air quotes from his manicured hands. "– 'Savior of Mankind;' and President William H. Taft the Extra Large, the *actual* savior of mankind."

The man smiles, his teeth glinting.

"All this and more, on this installment of ..."

A massive fireball erupts across the screen. A pair of words done up in burnished purple steel slam forward.

"... *Exponential Apocalypse!*"

CHAPTER ONE
MAKING MOVIES

"HEY, HI, I'D LIKE TO PLACE AN ORDER FOR DELIVERY?"

"Address?"

"888 88th Street, West New New –"

"Vicky?"

"... no?"

"Vicky, c'mon, you know we can't sell to yous two any–"

"We said we were sorry!"

"*You killed Justin.*"

"Yeah, but we paid for the funeral."

"I dunno if you understand how lucky you are that no one pressed charges."

"Like they even could've. We're in the penthouse, Sal. *The penthouse.* That couch was falling for a long, looong time before it hit him. And what was he doing in the dumpster anyway? A lot of this is on him."

"Justin wasn't *in* the dumpster, Vicky. He was *running away*. The couch was soaked wit' volatile chemicals and *exploded*."

"Well, yeah. Why do you think we were throwing it out?"

The man on the other end of the phone sighed heavily. "Look, we can't deliver to yous guys anymore, Vicky, full stop. I guess you could ... I dunno, come here and pick it up? I could pro–"

Queen Victoria XXX ended the call.

"Hel's crusty butthole," she mumbled. Tossing her cell phone onto the breakfast counter and returning to the living room, the woman in the Cheeto-stained t-shirt announced: "Bad news, buddy. We're blacklisted from Restaino's now, too."

"Damn it," grumbled her roommate, "they had the best pickles in the district!"

"I'm disappointed too."

"Why are people even still *using* humans for deliveries? A robot would have survived that blast, easy."

"I know," she sighed.

"This is bullshit," grumbled Thor.

Thor Odinson, Norse God of Thunder, and Queen Victoria XXX, the thirtieth and only extant clone of the original Queen Victoria, were living on the top floor of a swanky apartment building, built over the charred crater of the Holiday Inn they had, years earlier, called home. The lodging had been a covert and completely untraceable token of thanks from Ah Puch, the former Mayan God of Death, after the pair had helped to murder Ah Puch's former boss, Walt Sidney, an act that had resulted in the reins – and bank accounts, and gold stores, and goat farms – of Sidney's massive global entertainment conglomerate being handed to the Mesoamerican god.

The copied queen and the Scandinavian god had been so appreciative of the gesture, they decided to never leave the apartment – like, ever. Between the lack of mercenary work available and the seemingly unshakeable bouts of guilt and depression, going outside simply hadn't seemed worth the effort.

More importantly, they were rich and famous legends now and all their undiagnosed mental disorders were written off as fashionable eccentricities. Shut-ins across the globe were suddenly seen as hip and trendy.

That, dear reader, was how Thor found himself sitting in a plush velvet armchair in his own living room while a skinny man in a ballcap and a pretentiously-tied Afghan scarf paced behind him. A small woman with a clear plastic bag of makeup over her shoulder was perched in the god's lap, working an industrial-strength personal trimmer – the kind usually reserved for show ponies – all the way up the thunder god's nose.

The tiny machine made an increasingly desperate noise before finally giving up and stopping cold. The woman pulled the smoking hygienic instrument from the Norseman's nostril.

"That's the third one this morning," she grumbled.

"Maybe just leave my nose hairs alone then?"

Marlene Cage-Jones laughed, hard and derisively, then climbed off the big man.

"Sit tight," she said, patting his knee. "I've got something in the truck."

"Marlene?" asked the skinny man, Alfredo Trabaverga, watching as his makeup woman rushed to the door. "Where are you —"

The door slammed shut behind her.

With a noise that was mostly consonants, Alfredo buried his face in his hands. Around him, the rest of his film crew bustled – though they adamantly did not hustle – setting up lights and cameras, running cables, moving furniture, and kicking the candy wrappers and empty soda cans they were supposed to be cleaning up back under the moved furniture.

"Guys," he said, to no one in particular. "We need to get this done *today*. We are so far behind schedule already."

"That sounds like a *you* problem," said Queen Victoria XXX, flopping down onto the matching velvet chaise. Her previously meticulously coiffed hair was frizzy, and flattened on one side. She was wearing ratty sweatpants and one of Thor's old shirts, covered with her own new stains.

The tall woman stretched out across the lounge, putting her mismatched fuzzy socks on the edge of the armchair, dangerously close to her roommate's immaculately appareled arm. The wardrobe woman, Kelly Squatchson, swatted her feet away.

Thor, after all, was in a crisp, white Oxford with a red paisley necktie, both supplied by the production, and both brand new – a state in which Kelly intended them to remain. The big man had refused their offer of slacks, however, opting instead – and only after significant cajoling and bargaining, given that he wanted to do the interview in his underwear – for his own tattered jeans, more holes than pants at this point.

"Remind me why we're doing this again?" asked the thunder god, a finger up his nose, massaging his nasal membranes.

"Because the Neo-GOP's technomancers have made it impossible to teach history or share 'controversial' facts without being eaten alive by a swarm of nanolocusts. Therefore we have to do this entire fucking thing with actor reenactments and non-binding personal recollections."

"What thing?" asked the queen.

"How high are you?" asked the director.

"So very," she replied.

The director puffed out his cheeks and exhaled. "Taft has, in an effort to keep the world from sliding into Trumpian Era levels of stupidity and shortsighted shittiness, commissioned myself and my team to docudramatize all of the world's known history for a thirteen-part educational Netflix miniseries tentatively titled *The Exponential Apocalypses*. For reasons that I truly and *sincerely* do not understand, you two slackers have, somehow, been at the center of *at least* three-and-a-half of the last five apocalypses, and may have even had a hand in stopping them entirely." He shrugged, half-angrily and half-hopelessly. "So we're spending the last episode on you and whichever of your friends are still alive and willing to talk to us."

"OK ..." Thor slowly replied. "But *why* are *we* doing this?"

"Because the president," explained the redheaded assistant director, Harley Brochovich, walking by, "tricked you into signing an ironclad contract saying that you'd cooperate with us in a timely and helpful manner."

This was not hyperbole. The contract was literally carved into a slab of iron, locked in an iron box, and guarded by a team of iron men in iron masks. Thor and Queen Victoria XXX hadn't seen the document since they scratched their names into it with a diamond-tipped pen.

"Joke's on you guys, then," said the unkempt woman who was shortly supposed to be interviewed on camera. "We don't cooperate with *anyone*."

"Clearly," mumbled Alfredo.

"What if, though," suggested the assistant director, "we got you your sandwiches?"

"Are you trying to bribe us?" asked Thor.

"Yes," she replied, matter-of-factly.

"OK, good."

"We're listening," added Queen Victoria XXX. Across the room, the door opened and Marlene reentered the apartment, dragging a heavy, military-issued duffel bag behind her.

"How many sandwiches," said Harley, tapping away at the tablet strapped to her wrist, "would it take to get you to do this? To *properly* do this?"

"How big's your budget?" asked the replicated royal in reply.

"I'm gonna go make some room in the fridge," said Thor, putting his hands on the arms of his chair and pushing himself up.

"Not so fast," said the makeup woman, shoving him back down, her tiny hand nearly lost between the god's pecs. With a heave, Marlene tossed her duffel bag into his lap, then, digging, pulled out a butane welding torch and a ceramic combat knife.

"I am getting those fucking nose hairs out of there if it fucking kills me."

IN MEMORY OF

Marlene Cage-Jones, Makeup Woman

Rest in Peace
You're Plucking the Eyebrow Hairs of Angels Now

CHAPTER TWO
MARCH OF THE PENGUINS

"GUYS," PLEADED THE DIRECTOR. "COME ON."

The entirety of his crew was sitting around the gilded slice of redwood that acted as a coffee table, some on various parts of the crushed velvet furniture set, others on the unbelievably plush carpeting. Thor Odinson and Queen Victoria XXX, meanwhile, were seated atop the table, holding court, every one of their guests – except for Alfredo Trabaverga, obviously – hanging raptly on their every word.

After the tag team of a solar superstorm and volcanic winter had ended the world for the twenty-sixth and twenty-seventh times, respectively, the almost annual apocalypses that had been wrecking up the planet kind of just ... stopped. Suddenly faced with a lot more free time, buildings that stayed built, and money that actually meant something, society started relaxing and reading and, counter to almost everyone's expectations, *learning*.

There was, in fact, a resurgent Renaissance, with intelligence and creativity and science and art all actually valued again. Despite the rise of the Neo-GOP and their efforts to keep everyone scared and stupid, the vast majority of humanity got to book-learnin' and smart-makin', with the analysis and understanding of the causes and effects of recent history rapidly becoming a cornerstone of the movement. (There had been, after all, only so much one could learn about current events living their life out of a boarded-up basement.)

Of course, people were still people, and better stories often won out over facts and truth. Comic books and movies riddled with excessive explosions were always more popular than textbooks and dry documentaries. And Thor Odinson and Queen Victoria XXX, effortlessly charming and alarmingly pretty, unafraid to say what they meant and always willing to punch their way out of a problem, made for some great subjects.

That was how, despite a growing agoraphobia and a complete lack of doing anything anymore, the god and the queen found themselves elevated from respected black-market mercenaries to outright legends, known and loved by everyone.

"Union rules say you get *one* lunch," continued Alfredo.

"... so then the guy's all like –" Thor adopted a terrible British accent. "– since the ocean now reaches into the swamps, therefore the swamps and all that is built on top of them are, by royal degree, a part of the sovereign lands of Atlantis."

"So, of course," continued the queen, "I'm all like, fuck that noise, so I start wrapping the bike chain around my knuckles to punch this guy in his stupid face –"

"– when some crazy-ass radioactive swamp monster thing explodes out of the muck and bites his stupid fish head right off his stupid human body!"

The miniseries' crew erupted with laughter.

"Are you at least filming this?" asked the director. Hector Vanhanen-Vazquez, the cameraman, aggressively ignored him.

"The monster's still outside," continued Queen Victoria XXX, popping open another Dr. Pepper Cherry. "His name's Marv. Fucking *Marv*. He ended up getting the whole Meadowlands federally protected as culturally significant wetlands or whatever."

"And, oh, shit," said the thunder god, several bites of chicken parm in his mouth, "so this *other* time –"

A tremendous kersplosion – bigger than a regular explosion by about half, usually accompanied by a cartoonish fireball – rocked the apartment, the entire western wall reduced to pointy confetti and splintering across the living room.

"Bragi's grody razors," mumbled Thor, shoving the last of his sandwich into his mouth. His soda was soaking through his jeans and into his undershorts.

"That was my favorite wall!" added Queen Victoria XXX.

A teeming horde of the world's most adorable puppies and kittens – accompanied by a legion of piglets and fawns and a couple baby hedgehogs – wobbled through the ensuing dust cloud, bows in their hair and bandanas around their necks, yipping preciously, their tiny legs barely covering any ground at all.

"Ohhh," cooed Harley Brochovich. "They're so cute!"

"Stinkfarts," snarled the thunder god.

"... what?"

"*Stinkfarts*," he rumbled again, the floor around him quaking.

"That's not their real name," explained the queen, standing up and stretching. "That's what Thor calls them because they're dirty and smelly and they use a noxious chemical gas emitted from their hindquarters as a weapon. Speaking of, we have a bunch of gas masks in the hall closet. You're going to want them."

Alfredo, poking his head up from behind the sofa and noticing a distinct lack of movement from the burly blonde man and the lean, black-haired woman, asked: "And you ... don't?"

"Well, Thor's a god ..."

"And she's been living with me for two years," added Thor, "so she's built up an immunity to noxious gas."

"Awww, they don't look so scary," said one of the production assistants, kneeling down and putting out a hand, "they just need some love and maybe a bath and –"

The stinkfart farted, stinkily, releasing a cloud of opalescent green vapor that quickly enveloped the woman and began simultaneously choking her and melting off her skin from the inside out.

"*HOLY SHIT*," said basically everyone, the crew erupting into a complete panic.

"Not yet," Thor explained grimly.

"What?!" asked someone, shoving someone else out of their way.

"This gets worse?!" asked a third someone, backing toward the door.

"Like you wouldn't believe," continued the thunder god, stomping forward, grabbing one of the puppies by the scruff, and hurling it outside. "Stinkfarts are genetically engineered from bonnacons.[i] The gas is just a defense mechanism. The shit is the *actual* weapon."

"They wouldn't do this on their own, though," said Queen Victoria XXX, bringing her fuzzy sock-covered foot down on a kitten's head. "They're nowhere near capable of handling explosives and surviving."

"Then who ..."

As the dust surrounding the hole settled, the answer to that half-finished question became abundantly clear.

Penguins.

Motherfucking penguins.

At least a dozen, old and grizzled, with bright blue sweatbands around their heads, fully-armed and waddling closer. Behind them, several helicopters were hovering, another one dropping down and lining itself up with the hole in the wall. Two-foot-tall shit golems began pouring out and into the penthouse, seemingly gloating over the fact that they were walking piles of poo.

"Not the rug!" shouted the clone.

"That is never coming out," echoed the god.

The assortment of tiny terrors – making sure to run across the furniture on their way – laid into the crowd of confused crew members, pouncing and biting and hitting and farting. Immediately, a dark stain spread across the crotchular area of the stoned queen's sweatpants.

"Oh, thank God, you're scared too," said Harley, cowering behind the armchair. "That makes me feel –"

"No, not even a little," replied Queen Victoria XXX, her face like granite. "Fear is for idiots. I just needed to get the drugs out of my system. This was the easiest way."

"Isn't that a little ... *gross*, though?"

"We're fighting dookie demons, lady," said Thor, his arm outstretched. "This is going to get so much grosser." Mjolnir, the god's enchanted hammer, busted through an interior wall and sailed into his hand.

"*Thor*," scolded the queen.

"What? We'll tell the insurance company these assholes did it." He turned to Hector, now fervently filming. "Don't put that part in the documentary." The cameraman gave Thor a thumbs up.

"Docudrama," added the director, leaning out from behind the cameraman.

A penguin with spiked nunchucks tottered menacingly toward the retired heroes, swinging his weapons this way and that, whipping the points through the air in a demonstration of his awe-inspiring abilities. Queen Victoria XXX kicked the bird back through the hole in the wall and directly into the rotor of one of the helicopters. The flying machine listed downward and exploded against one of the lower floors, sending a shudder through the building.

"Whoops."

"Also not in the film!" the Norseman shouted. "Here, try again."

He grabbed one of the stinkfarts and tossed it to his roommate. She spiraled the hedgehog through the windshield of another copter, the creature rupturing into guts and quills against the pilot's face. The helicopter reared sideways into another helicopter, which, in turn, got its blades tangled up with those from a third helicopter. All three twisted, smoking, to the ground, erupting in a tremendous fireball.

"That should be OK," said the god, "depending on what they landed on."

"I hope it wasn't Marv," added the queen.

One of the little shits flooding the room hopped off the boom operator it was teabagging and chirped shrilly. The rest of the golems did the same, then pulled lighters from inside of themselves and, with a ritualistic series of hand movements, set themselves on fire.

"Balls," grumbled Thor. "This one's on me. I recognize these guys now."

"From that time –"

"Yeah."

"With the –"

"Yeah," confirmed the thunder god. "Maybe I didn't kill them enough the first time."

"Clearly," said the queen. She nodded her head toward the grip getting beaten about the face by a penguin with a cricket bat. "We should probably get them out of here, right?"

Thor shrugged. "You do you, Vicky."

"Maybe later," she said, a flash in her eyes. "We'll see how tired I am."

"Well, if there's anything I can do to help –"

"Yo, dawg," screeched one of the penguins, a voice like Styrofoam fingernails being dragged across a Styrofoam chalkboard, "we heard you like saving the world." The bird pulled an absurdly complicated tangle of wires and circuit boards and glowing tubes from a backpack.

"Fuck," said Thor.

"These aren't regular evil penguins, are they?"

"Try saving it from *this!*" squawked another penguin.

"OK," said the thunder god, stomping toward the Antarctic birds, "sure."

Immediately, he was swarmed by the flaming poo creatures.

"Baldur's ass crack!" The Norseman swung his arms, his hammer, impotently, cutting through the flaming crap demons only to have the golems reform. "Why are you so soft?!" he shouted. "Are you not getting enough iron?"

Queen Victoria XXX, meanwhile, kicked a baby deer in the face. Then she got smacked in her own face by Alfredo Trabaverga.

"What the actual *fuck*," she rumbled, turning toward him.

"AAHHAAHHAAHH!" cried the director. "AAAHHH!" The skinny man was swaying wildly, his arms flailing weakly, as a pair of penguins tried to, respectively, choke him to death with his scarf and saw through his neck with an expensive steak knife.

"You're supposed to be cute and cuddly!" he screeched.

"And that is exactly why we are doing this!" shouted the first penguin. "No one takes us seriously! We have the technological capacity to melt the ice caps, condense an atomic bomb into a child's school bag, create a black hole machine, harness the power of undersea magma flows, *and* talk with perfect human accents, and all you want to do is make documentaries about how great and adorable we are!"

"*We are not cute, you fissured asshole!*" shouted the second bird, stabbing the steak knife deep into Alfredo's trapezius. The director screamed incoherently and fell to the floor.

"Wait," said Queen Victoria XXX, grabbing the penguins by the tail and holding them upside down, "you're here because of the documentary guys? Not us?"

"They're documentarians?!" screeched another bird altogether.

"Docudramatists, actually," the director wheezed. "We're not legally allowed to –"

"*KILL THEM ALL!*"

"Why are you saying that like it wasn't already your plan?" asked Thor, grabbing the screeching waterfowl by the head and crushing its skull between his fingers.

The two penguins in the clone's hands squawked in horror, wriggling in her grip. Queen Victoria XXX clonked their heads together and then bowled them out of the apartment. She looked back at her roommate.

Through a disgusting series of trials and errors, the thunder god had discovered that the stinkfarts could damage the shit golems and vice versa, allowing him, via the prodigious misuse of weaponized feces, to successfully defeat both offending parties.

The apartment, amazingly, was none the worse for wear after the endeavor.

Thor, however, was another story entirely.

"You look like –"

"Don't, Vicky."

"Oh, come on!" she implored, hopping slightly. "When else am I ever going to get to say that and actually *literally* mean it."

"You hate puns," he countered.

"I'll let you watch later."

The thunder god raised an eyebrow. "You were saying, then?"

"You look like –"

A whir and a sound of distant popping filled the apartment. Across the room, a trio of penguins in white lab coats and giant glasses had finished activating the bomb. The laws of physics started to act kind of weird.

"*Motherfucker,*" grumbled Thor, gravity rapidly losing a hold on him. "Any ideas?"

"Implosion bomb is my guess," the queen replied, her feet drifting from the floor.

"So I can –"

"Go nuts."

"Your iPod and stuff in the rubber-reinforced safe?"

"Yeah," she replied, backhanding a nearing penguin into two others – and sending herself backwards along the way. "Maybe, like, now, though," she added, thudding into a decorative column.

The thunder god turned to the cameraman. "Hope you got a long lens, 'cause you're gonna want to be in the hallway for this."

Hector nodded and shoved off an armchair, floating gently toward the front door, changing lenses as he went.

Outside, the sky turned black with roiling clouds. The last of the helicopters began twitching as the growing electromagnetic forces in the air started messing with all the parts that make helicopters fly. A colossal lightning bolt ripped through the sky, pulled a sharp ninety-degree turn, and cannonballed horizontally in between the careening choppers, through the broken wall and straight into the jury-rigged bomb – as well as the two avian assholes standing over it.

There was a blinding flash, thunder that shook the entire block, and then the walls were splattered with chunks of penguin scientists.

Harley Brochovich, floating along the ceiling, vomited at the sight. Things did not end well for her.

"Gross," said Thor, looking up.

"Uh, hey, buddy," said Queen Victoria XXX, floating past and pointing a thumb toward the whirring doomsday machine. "That thing's still working."

"Not for long it's not."

"Please hurry," choked Harley.

Tossing Mjolnir and holding onto the handle, the God of Thunder glided across the room, the hammer – and then Thor – slamming hard into the pile of electronics. Nothing seemed to break. Furrowing his brow, the Norseman grabbed the bomb and, counterbalancing himself with his magic cudgel, hurled the bomb with everything he had, through the hole in the wall, through the crack he had years ago made in the sky, and into outer God damned space.

"And now it's gone forever," said Thor, wiping his hands clean.

Everything collided with the ground at once.

"Can I ... Can I get a paper towel or something," mumbled Harley, rolling onto her back. "Maybe, like, a lot?"

"Oh, come on, it's all over the carpet now!" scolded Queen Victoria XXX.

"So," said the thunder god, covered in shit and penguin guts and lifting up Alfredo Trabaverga by his armpit, "you still want to ask us those questions for your *Exponential Apocalypse* show or what?"

"The *Exponential Apocalyps*-es," the director croaked.

Thor made a face. "Pretty sure mine's better, man."

"*What did you do to your clothes?!*" screamed Kelly Squatchson.

IN THEIR OWN WORDS

ON THE SCREEN: HARRISON CHRISTOPHER, AN UNAGING HALF-angel, half-man, is dressed in a bespoke dark blue suit. Every crease is perfect. The camera tightens on his golden-hued visage, head tilted at the exact right angle to indicate deep wells of compassion and curiosity, but also leaning forward just enough to let everyone know that *he* is the one asking the questions, that he can make or break a reputation with a single word. His eyes twinkle, like stars above an endless desert.

"So, Thor, former Scandinavian Lord of Thunder," the host begins, smiling genially, "the man who cracked the sky to save the world, but then did nothing to stop Nikola Tesla's earthquake machine, but then reinvigorated the continental grid and saved us again, but also killed beloved children's entertainment icon Walt Sidney, tell us: Why?"

"What?" asks the thunder god, raising an eyebrow. He's classically handsome, like a statue from antiquity come to life, only sexier and paler. His golden hair is pulled back into a half-ponytail, his beard looks like that of a lumberjack winning an award. His dark blue chambray shirt is tight, threatening to explode off of him.

"Why did you kill Walt Sidney?"

"Are we really doing this again? I already told you –"

The subtlest of cuts. Thor's head shifts positions ever-so-slightly.

"– I killed Walt Sidney because he pit Satan, your Judeo-Christian Devil, against Loki, the Norse God of Being a Dick – and, also, my half-brother – to see who could kill my friends Mark and Timmy first. In the process, Catrina ..."

Thor pauses, looks away. His eyes unfocus.

"Catrina ..." leads the host.

"You know what?" says the Norseman, squinting his eyes and shaking his head. "Fuck this." The big man stands up, his big crotch, barely contained by his sweatpants, taking up most of the frame. "I'm out of here."

"You can't ..." stammers Harrison from off-screen. "Is he allowed to do this?"

As Thor's midsection stomps past the edge of the armchair, a blurry Queen Victoria XXX can be seen walking out of the bathroom at the other end of the room, waving her hand behind her. The camera focuses as best it can.

"Nobody go in there for a while," she says. "I think that Thai I had for breakfast went bad. Like, a couple days ago."

***

"So, you and Thor," continues Harrison Christopher, the twinkle in his eye becoming downright lascivious. "You've been sharing a home together for the better part of two years. What's that like?"

"What's what like?" asks Queen Victoria XXX, her voice like dragged concrete. She looks like she was genetically engineered to simultaneously be the most beautiful and most dangerous woman alive – because she was. Multi-ethnic to the point that it doesn't matter anymore, her skin is dark and flawless. She has the face of a model, the shoulders of an Olympic swimmer, and the glare of a lion tamer that left her bag of fucks-to-give at home.

"I assume there have to have been some ... *misunderstandings?*" continues the host.

"Never."

"After the death of your husband, Chester Arthur Arthur the –"

"He wasn't my husband," she says. "And the A wasn't for another Arthur." A pause. "Did you *seriously* think it was Chester Arthur *Arthur?*"

"With him gone," continues Harrison, "you must have felt ... well, *lonely*, right?"

"Not right."

"Come on now, Vicky –"

"You can call me Your Majesty."

"– there had to be certain things that you missed about him?"

"Did I miss things about the man I loved?" The queen looks off camera. "You're actually paying this asshole?"

"What kind of things?" the host presses, unabated.

"Well, Thor and I are terrible with money for one thing." She sneers. "And neither of us can cook –"

"Of course, of course, but what about certain ... *bedroom* things?"

"Oh, we have a maid for that now. We broke the washing machine on, like –"

"Maybe I'm not making myself clear."

Queen Victoria XXX smiles at the man sitting opposite her, her mouth not matching any other part of her.

"No," she says, "you're making yourself *very* clear."

Her eyes flash. At the bottom edge of the screen, the queen, almost imperceptibly, moves her arm, dropping it along the side of the armchair.

"Let me be more direct, then," says Harrison Christopher, tenting his fingers and leaning forward. "What I'm asking is, did you and Thor ever – Fuck! Where did you –"

An abrupt camera switch.

"Let me show you how *I* interview people," says the clone, rising from the chair, an enormous hunting knife in her hand, the blade reflecting the lights into the camera.

Smash cut to black.

***

A scene already in progress. The image is shaky and blurry as the cameraman tries to get everything into focus.

"– not good enough for you, man? Huh?" shouts a scrawny, Middle Eastern hippie. He looks like he's auditioning for the lead in *Jay & Silent Bob: The Musical.* "They get all the glory, the screen time?"

"Jesus Christ," mumbles a redheaded woman behind him.

"What?!" roars the skinny man, turning on her.

Tom Petty's "You Don't Know How It Feels" starts playing, then stops almost immediately, abruptly, almost as if the docudrama couldn't secure the rights.

"Yo," says Jesus Christ into his phone, eyes like the sky after a hurricane locked on the assistant director.

"Uh-huh," he continues.

His brow creases in concern. He breaks contact with the redhead, looking toward the ground, and starts pacing absentmindedly.

"Laced with what?" he asks.

"And? What d'you mean '*and*?" he asks again.

"Uh-huh."

"Well, damn. OK."

"Thanks?"

The Judeo-Christian Savior of Mankind slides his cell phone back into his pocket.

"Uh, sorry," he says, turning, in turn, and then back again, to Harley Brochovich and the camera. "Sorry. Truly. That wasn't – I gotta – Look, I gotta go take care of something real fast. Do you guys have, like, a medic on hand?" He stumbles behind a nearby trailer. "Are they down here?"

"How in *the fuck* did these guys save the planet?" grumbles Alfredo Trabaverga, pulling off his ballcap and rubbing his forehead with his one working hand.

"We've technically still got the reenactors for –" Harley scrolls through the tablet on her arm. "– another two weeks, if you want –"

"Yeah. Call 'em. I'll get in touch with the studio, have them get in touch with Taft. I think we got ten minutes of useable footage with these clowns."

"There wasn't a medic back there," says Jesus Christ, reemerging from behind the trailer. "Can, uh, can one of you give me a ride to a hospital? Or something?"

CHAPTER THREE

CAN YOU SPOT ALL THE MARVEL COMICS REFERENCES?

FOUR-AND-A-HALF HOURS AFTER THE DOCUDRAMA STARTED, THE episode's end credits *finally* rolled, intercut with bloopers from the production, most of them involving the mostly-naked British Indian reenactor and some version of Chris Pratt.

"I have *a lot* of issues with what we just watched," said Queen Victoria XXX, fully-clothed in pink flannel pajamas, on the floor and leaning against the bottom of the sofa.

"Why'd they make me a fat white guy?" asked Jesus Christ, also on the floor, also in pink flannel pajamas, and reaching for his bong.

"British is literally the *one* nationality that I'm not," continued the genealogically-muddled clone. "I mean, yeah, there's *some* Queen Victoria in there, but just the German stuff."

"I don't think I'm fat," said the Prince of Peace, holding his breath. "Am I fat?"

"And, look, I get that the Chris Pratts are contractually obligated to be in literally every film production across the globe, but, *come on*, Charlie was *not* a Chris Pratt type. A Chris Evans, *maybe*."

"*That's* the Chris Pratt you have an issue with in that thing?"

"I don't know, I liked it," said Thor Odinson with a shrug, sprawled in a bathrobe on the couch behind them.

"Then you," said the Judeo-Christian Son of God, exhaling and returning the now weedless bong to the coffee table, "can get the rest of us more beer."

"And whiskey," added the queen.

"And a couple of Cokes."

"And maybe make some coffee."

"Also, we're out of Bugles."

"The rest ..." repeated the Norse Son of Odin, scrunching his face. "It is just you two, right?"

"I bring *one* invisible woman home," said the queen, "and all of a sudden —"

Led Zeppelin's "Immigrant Song" starting blaring from Thor's terrycloth pocket. The beefy blondie fished for his phone.

"Hello?" he said, his giant fingers accidentally putting the call on speaker.

"Why in the ever-loving *fuck* did you throw it into space?!" shouted the voice on the other end, roaring like an arachnophobic newspaper editor. "And why, in the ever-loving-er fuck, did you throw it into the *scientifically-impossible dimensional rift* you created five years ago?!"

"Oh, so it's *my* fault you haven't fixed that yet?"

"Hey, Billy," hollered Queen Victoria XXX.

"Couldn't you have just smashed it?!" continued the president, his roar degenerating into a whine. "What happened to 'Thor smash computery thing?'"

"Man, I tried," explained Thor. "Didn't you watch the docuwhatever?"

"We're fucked, Thor. The entire world is *fucked.*"

"How fucked?"

The man on the phone grumbled. "Just meet me at the White House."

"The original or the fake one that sells waffles?"

"Oh, shit, we're getting waffles?" asked Jesus. "Forget the Bugles then, man. Where are my shoes?"

CHAPTER FOUR

IT'S JUST A JUMP TO THE LEFT

AFTER THE LAS VEGAS MASSACRE REDUCED THE WORLD'S MOST prosperous city to rubble, a burning, itching desire for a new, centralized government spread across the globe like a particularly virulent strain of gonorrhea – in no small part because the city-state of Las Vegas had, in fact, being doing almost all of the heavy lifting for the entire planet, sending supplies and money and people wherever they were needed, and keeping society afloat all by its lonesome.

With the city now destroyed – and much like a toddler with a handgun – humanity quickly proved that it couldn't be left alone without supervision.

With fires still firing and disasters still disastering – albeit in significantly less planet-ravaging ways – it didn't take long for every extant nation and territory on the planet to unite, voluntarily and enthusiastically, under the firm and calloused – yet tender and dexterous – hand of William H. Taft XLII. The forty-second and only-surviving clone of the twenty-seventh president of the former United States of America was unanimously elected Benevolent Dictator of Situations and Mankind, with everyone agreeing that, even though the Las Vegas Massacre had occurred under his watch, he clearly must have learned a thing or two about not allowing vast swaths of people to die gruesomely.

Unified for the first time, a massive rebranding effort soon swept across the globe like a curler on speed. The island of North America,ⁱⁱ a motley collection of city-states and independent territories and truck stops, became the united country of New Springsteen – named after the singer-songwriter and hero of the Third Robot War – and was quickly chosen to be the presiding nation of the Federation of All Residents of Terra and Surrounding Space Stations.

The city of Washington, D.C., meanwhile, was selected as the planet's capitol and rebuilt,[iii] right down to the historic monuments and the White House – except this time all the statues of slaveholders and sexual predators were left out, the White House was given a more inclusive coat of paint, the city was relocated to the newly-constructed junk island of New New York, and it wasn't actually called Washington, D.C. anymore.

Similarly, the rechristened Rainbow House – also being rebuilt from scratch, the original White House having been gilded during, and then melted down after, the disastrous presidency of Donald "Jerkface" Trump – was updated with a host of modern settings, including laser fences and a dinosaur garden, because there was a time to stand on ceremony and tradition, and there was a time to install a holographic fantasy dome in the basement.

"Mark, Timmy," said Thor Odinson, nodding toward the two squirrels scampering across the floor and up a potted tree as he entered the Rainbow House's Octagonal Office. Behind the burly blonde man were Queen Victoria XXX and Jesus Christ, all three of them looking as though they'd just been disturbed from a lengthy nap. Doritos crumbs were falling out of both sons of gods' beards, while Vicky had simply thrown a leather jacket over her pajamas. All of them were wearing slippers.

William H. Taft XLII, meanwhile, was standing behind his desk, his jacket off, his sleeves rolled up, his tie half undone. His close-cropped hair, his Rooseveltian mustache, were going grey. A big man by all definitions of the term, he was resting his sledgehammer fists atop the desk and leaning his gorilla shoulders forward.

"Do you," he rumbled without looking up, "have *any* idea how bad you just screwed us all?"

"Nope," replied Thor.

"That thing you threw into space?" continued the president, now glaring at the trio. "That was a *black hole generator*. And you *hurled it into a crack* in the *you damned sky!* Do you know what it did when it got there? Do you? Do you know what the *black hole generator* did when you threw it into an *extradimensional hole*?"

"Explode ... ?" replied the thunder god.

"No, Thor, it did not explode. Want to try again?"

"Not really, no."

"The black hole generator, Thor, *generated a black fucking hole.*"

"That's bad, right?" asked Thor.

"Sounds pretty bad, brother," said Jesus Christ.

"You literally sentenced the entire planet to death!" explained William H. Taft XLII.

"OK, sure," said the Norseman, "but you've said that before."

"*But this time I said literally!*" He slammed his fist into the desk hard enough to splinter the wood. The veins on the president's neck looked like a slow-motion pipe-bomb, bulging and fractions of moments away from tearing apart.

"Look, don't get your panties in a wad, Billy, all right?" said Queen Victoria XXX. "We're here. What do you need us to do?"

"You don't *do* anything," said the BDSM of FARTSSS, suddenly exhausted and crashing down into his chair. "I just wanted to yell at you in person."

"What? What do you mean, *nothing?*"

"I didn't – I didn't actually say 'nothing' ..."

"There's got to be *something*, though, right?" continued the queen. "Some crackpot with a crazy whatever-or-other in his basement? I mean, aren't we Renaissancing? Didn't you reinstate the mad scientists of Las Máquinas?"

"'Reinstate' is a little strong," said the president, leaning forward. He began rifling through papers and swiping through touch screens on his desk. "But I did issue a large number of grants for independent research on some pretty weird shit."

"Well, there you go," said Thor. Then: "So is this something we stay here and talk to you about? Or do we have to go to the Department of Science or something? Because there's a hot dog cart outside and –"

"We are not legally allowed to have that."

"The hot dog cart? That seems strict."

"We literally just saw it outside, man," added Jesus Christ.

"No, the Science Department," explained the big man, still searching. "The government is legally barred from having one."

Thanks to President Donald "Junk in the Trunk" Trump's recently unearthed Greatest Amendment You Ever Seen™, scientists (or anyone with more than a GED) were not permitted to work for or be funded by any iteration of any government presiding over any part of the land that previously housed the United States of America. The last president the America had ever had had had the U.S. Constitution reprinted on a sheet of solid gold and hand-carved the new amendment into the metal himself.

The addition was horribly misspelled and kind of *super* racist, but, still, somehow, it was law. As a result, scientists became entirely privately funded, through large corporate donations and viewers like you!

"But you *are* the government," said Queen Victoria XXX.

"It's a long story," said the president, pulling open drawers, "but give me five minutes and I can point you in something resembling the right direct–"

Suddenly, everyone was standing two feet farther forward than they had been less than a moment earlier. Thor had a hot dog in his mouth and two in each hand.

"What the shit," he mumbled, spewing bread chunks.

"Damn it," said the president, leaning against his desk, his arms crossed over his chest. "The hole's getting bigger than I thought."

"That's what she said."

"This isn't a joke."

"Yeah, I know," said the thunder god, "but what I said was."

"Black holes don't just affect space and physics, idiot, they can fuck with time too. And this one? I don't know if it was the bomb itself or the energies from the other dimension or what, but this one's acting all kinds of bananas – and it looks like we're all about to learn the specifics firsthand." William H. Taft XLII handed them the index card he was already holding in his hand, apparently. "Here. Go. Now. Try and fix this before we all die."

"So we *can* fix this?" asked Jesus Christ, his mouth also full of hot dog.

"No, that's why I said 'try,'" he replied. "Are you guys even listening?"

CHAPTER FIVE
TOO RA LOO RYE AYE

THOR ODINSON, QUEEN VICTORIA XXX, AND JESUS CHRIST stepped off the bus and stood marveling at a repurposed multi-level warehouse in one of the trendiest sections of the gleaming metropolis of New New York, D.C. The exterior of the building was painted, meticulously and thoroughly, in yellow-and-black plaid. Old Halloween and Christmas decorations hung in the windows, even though it was April, all holidays had been rolled into a single Holiday Day Week mega-event years ago, and Santa Claus had been presumed dead for decades.

"This is a science facility?" asked Queen Victoria XXX.

"This doesn't look like a science facility," answered Thor.

Thick vines of fairy lights surrounded the entryway, illuminating the glinting metal sign proclaiming this to be the home of Dexy's Midnight Astrophysicists.

"I think I sold these guys drugs once," said Jesus Christ.

"I think you might've sold them too many," said the queen.

"So do we knock," asked the thunder god, "or is this a —"

The automatic door before them opened automatically.

"Nevermind," he mumbled dejectedly.

The trio entered, walking through the wide, unguarded lobby, past topiaries of unicorns and frogs and trees, then took the freight elevator up a floor. The doors opened. A frenzied flurry of folks in lab coats were running around with their hands over their heads, like a bunch of post-doctoral Kermit the Frogs.

"This probably isn't great," said Queen Victoria XXX.

Thor grabbed the arm of the nearest person racing past and spun the man around to face them. The guy was young and reasonably attractive, except for his ridiculous high-fade pompadour. The name tag on his coat said Dr. Vanilla Ice II.

"Culsu's cooooch," groaned the queen, throwing her head back.
"What," said Thor, "you know this guy?"
"You don't? You love shitty music."

Following the gratuitous murders of the scientists of Las Máquinas by Loki Laufeyjarson, Norse God of Sucking Real Hard, and because of the success and popularity of Queen Victoria XXX, William H. Taft XLII, and their fellow faux federal friends, a huge number of the world's greatest scientific minds were cloned and uploaded into the also-cloned bodies of celebrities, in an effort to make science sexier and more appealing to the young folk.

Unfortunately for everyone, however, several teams of lawyers got involved and society's hopes for an actually intelligent Matt Damon were dashed. Because of the fear of litigation, only C-list or lower celebrities were used in the scientific experiment, since there was less chance they'd sue – or, more accurately, since they wouldn't be able to afford the *good* lawyers that were already up in the cloning company's business.

In the end, Xerox[iv] sold off the artificially apt actors and musicians and Kardashians to the highest bidders, the facsimile famous people now toiling away for corporations and special interests, slaving over test tubes and overclocked computers and remote weather stations, desperately looking for ways to improve the human condition, to understand the mysteries of the universe, and to make a massive profit off the results.

"We's all gonna die, yo!" explained Dr. Ice, trying – and failing – to pull free of Thor's grip. "There's a black hole, son! And it's expanding right at us!"

"Yeah," said the thunder god, "no shit. That's why we're here."

"How do we stop it?" asked Queen Victoria XXX, grabbing the man's other arm.

"Stop it?" said the imitation one-hit-wonder. "Bitch, I don't –"

The queen slapped him, hard, right across his stupid face.

"Motherf–" said Vanilla Ice II, stretching his jaw, his cheek red and already swelling. "I mean, sorry, yo. Residual misogyny from the cloning and all that."

"Yeah, no, I get it. Took me forever to stop wanting jellied eels."

"Then why'd you hit me?"

She shrugged. "I wasn't gonna *not* hit you."

"Can we get back to the black hole thing?" asked a visibly tense Jesus Christ. Around him, scientists continued to run and scream and cry and poop themselves and desperately make out with one another on top of desks. "There's a weird energy in here, brother, and it's starting to freak me out."

"Man, what's there to know? Black holes is bas'c'lly super deep gravity wells, right? Sucking up all light and matter and what-nots. Only the hyperbolic trajectory is replaced by the event horizon, meaning none of what's sucked up can escape back out."

"Obviously," said Thor.

"This one, though," continued the scientist, shaking his head. "We's reas'ably sure there's a huge, diseased asshole of a *quasar* on the flip side of the dimensional rift. Prolly why we ain't been able to identify nothing yet 'bout what it really is. Short version? This honkie's growing faster than black holes is supposed to grow, and with augmented and uncharacteristic effects. We –"

In less than a fraction of a fraction of a second, several more scientists-slash-washed-up-musicians were standing behind Dr. Ice. Jesus Christ, meanwhile, was outside, already half a joint deep into his relaxation exercises.

"Shit, yeah, just like that, yo," said Vanilla Ice II. "I guess."

"OK ..." said Queen Victoria XXX, looking around and making sure all of her parts were still there, "but, again, how do we stop it?"

"Man, wasn't you listening?"

"Apparently not," said Thor.

"Look, homegirl," said Dr. MC Hammer IV, "we don't know, y'dig? We've only been hired to study black holes for their potential effects on weight loss. And this one ... Well, 'wack as shit' has been coming up a lot around the office."

"Yeah," agreed Dr. Ice, "but we's gonna be *rich* as shit after the bonus for this clears, though!"

"You, uh, you know we're all going to die, right?" asked Queen Victoria XXX.

"Didn't you *just* tell us that?" added Thor.

"Nah, man. *You*, yeah. But me? I'mma be too rich to die."

"That's not how money works."

"Says you."

"Says anyone with even a modicum of financial, or common, sense," explained the queen. "I'm beginning to feel like we might need a second opinion here."

"Beginning?" parroted Thor.

"Here," said MC Hammer IV, placing a flash drive in her hand, "take this. This is all our documentation. We don't have the resources to do anything other than prove this is happening. If you want results, or options, or ... *hope*, you'll have to take our research elsewhere, somewhere that's too legit to quit ... on doing the requisite investigatory steps into finding a viable solution."

"Ooh! Ooh!" hooted Thor, jumping up and down.

"What? No. Whatever you're thinking," said Queen Victoria XXX, "no."

"What if I go into space and electrocute the black hole?"

"*Fuck no*, man!" added Vanilla Ice.

"But it might work!"

"It absolutely will *not* work, son. That's not how black holes black hole!"

"Besides," added Queen Victoria XXX, "we're not going into space, Thor."

"But I *wa*-nna," he whined.

"Look, I've been there, buddy. It's not great."

The scientists behind the other scientists began behaving in a much more X-rated fashion than previously. Tables and counters were being knocked clear; red lace was being thrown over the lighting fixtures.

"You guys should, uh, you should probably leave," said Dr. Hammer, eyeing his co-workers and sliding off his lab coat. "None of us know how to panic correctly, and, well, things're about to get real dirty up in here."

"Hey," replied the queen, putting a hand on his shoulder, "orgies are completely acceptable responses to panic, okay? Don't let anyone tell you otherwise."

"You's two's more than welcome to join us, then," said Vanilla Ice II, hopping on one foot as he pulled off his shoe.

"Let's not go that far," she countered.

***

The god, the queen, and the demigod sat on the curb outside the research facility, passing a joint between them. Multicolored lights strobed in the windows behind them, while bass thumped loud enough that they could feel it from the sidewalk.

Queen Victoria XXX fiddled absentmindedly with the flash drive in her hand.

"We need scientists," she said.

"Those were scientists," said Thor.

"We need *good* scientists."

"Aren't all the good ones dead?" asked Jesus Christ.

"Yeah, but can't you ..." The queen groaned, then put her arms out straight, mimicking a Frankenstein, despite thinking she was mimicking a zombie.

"The time for that was a couple years ago, sister," he explained. "Now? You're only gonna get a lot of gross and not a lot of helpful."

"Well, that's —" began the dark-haired clone, cutting herself off and hopping to her feet. "Wait. Good might be off the table, but good *enough* is still an option."

"What does that mean?" asked Thor. "Are we going to another nerd orgy? 'cause that one —" He pointed a thumb over his shoulder. "— got weird, *fast*, and that's coming from me."

CHAPTER SIX
MEET THE JETSONS

"Hi!" said Judy Lin, Scientist-in-Chief at Consolidated Phukital, opening the door to her office. She poked her head into the hallway. "Where's everyone else?"

"Dead," said Queen Victoria XXX grimly.

"Oh. That's a bummer," replied the scientist. "So it's ... just you two then?"

"Yeah," said Thor. "Well, us and Jesus, but he's not –"

"Are you guys ... *you know* ..." The woman in the white coat made some very confusing motions with her fingers.

"Uh, no ...?"

"Why does everyone keep asking that?" asked the cloned queen.

"Because of the Global Repopulation Effort," the scientist answered severely.

"I thought that was voluntary."

"OK, sure," she scoffed. "If you want humanity to end."

"Hey, funny story ..." said Thor.

***

"Well?" asked Queen Victoria XXX. She was standing behind Judy, who, in turn, was standing in front of a computer, hunched over and waaay too close to the screen.

Judy Lin was on the smaller side – though most women were, compared to the part-Amazonian Queen Victoria XXX – and appeared to have undergone some kind of plastic surgery since the last time the clone had seen her. Or maybe she'd simply healed. At any rate, the scientist, formerly of the Amalgamated Provinces and States of Canada, America, and Mexico's Department of Science, was no longer wearing a bag over her head to hide her massive disfigurement at the hands – and feet, and at least one elbow – of an atomic werewolf that she'd helped create.

Turned out, she was kind of plain-looking.

"We won't know for sure for another day or two ... We need to compile some more of this data, double-check our opportunity windows, but ..." The scientist paused for an unseemly amount of time.

"But?"

"Preliminarily," she said, standing up straight, "we could shoot Thor into space."

"Yes!" shouted Thor, raising his hands over his head.

"No!" shouted the queen. "How would that even –"

"We have a rocket in the warehouse," said Judy, pointing a thumb toward the back of the laboratory. "We've been working on a time-quickening quantum core to counteract the effects of a black hole, you know, for fun. But we haven't been able to come up with a strong enough power source to make it go boom."

"I understood most of that ..."

"You can't *stop* a black hole. The only thing you can do is wait one out. Over time, a black hole will fill up and evaporate, like spaghetti in a sink drain. Though, obvs, we don't have that kind of time – or the ability to not get absorbed in the meanwhile. I mean, unless we do. You guys have been jumping through time, right?"

"We have," said Thor.

"Well, maybe, if we wait long enough ... the extradimensional energy ... will ... speed us up to a point ... where ... we've already figured all of this out?" The scientist looked around the room. "No? What about ... backwards? To give us more time?" She looked at her watch. "Hm. What about ... now? ... Now! ... No? OK, what about –"

"Judy, I feel like we're getting off topic," said the queen.

"Oh, really? 'cause I don't."

"You want to send Thor into space because ..."

"Because if he can detonate the quantum core, we can speed up time around the black hole and force the singularity to disappear, *without* destroying the planet," explained the tiny woman. "Even better, Thor's an ageless god, so he won't grow super old and die and decay if he gets caught up in the blast radius."

"What was your plan before me?" questioned the god in question.

"A dangerous amount of hydrogen bombs. And Owen." She glared across the lab toward another scientist. "He's a dick."

"Huh."

"Well, shit," said Queen Victoria XXX, suddenly feeling heavy. She sank into a nearby rolling chair. "I guess you *are* going into space."

"I mean, unless that Jesus guy you keep going on about figures out something better," said Judy. "The math on this is *wildly* theoretical."

CHAPTER SEVEN
GOD ONLY KNOWS

JESUS CHRIST KNOCKED ON THE D—

Jesus Christ was standing in his father's living room.

"I am really starting to dislike that," he mumbled.

Amen-Ra, former Egyptian God-King of the Sun, a.k.a. Odin, former Norse All-Father, a.k.a. God, a.k.a. Zeus, a.k.a. Jupiter, a.k.a. everyone else, was sitting on a well-worn recliner in his bathrobe, heart-adorned boxing shorts, and threadbare slippers, watching the Weather Channel. On the screen, an ancient Jim Cantore was placidly explaining that he was getting word that there appeared to be a black hole just beyond the earth's atmosphere, and that that wasn't good. There was probably going to be a lot of rain for one thing, along with unpredictable tides. Strong winds and earthquakes were also possible, depending on how fast the planet's rotation slowed. And – obviously this went without saying, he said – but all of humankind was probably going to die horribly, and soon.

"Oh, so you know," said Jesus, leaning over and kissing his father's bald head.

"Yes," said Amen-Ra.

"Any chance you could, you know, fix this?"

"I'm retired, son."

"So are Thor and Vicky, but they're still out there, trying."

"Well, Thor has never exactly had the strongest convictions, now has he?"

"The planet's kinda ... *doomed*, Dad."

"It's been doomed before."

"I know, but –"

"Humanity, penguinkind, the sasquatches and the merfolk and all the rest who have tried this nonsense before ..." Ra waved his hand dismissively. "No one is going to learn anything if we keep interfering, if we keep saving them from themselves."

"Yeah, I remember," growled Jesus Christ, instinctively pulling his hands together, running a thumb across the scar on the opposite palm. "But what happened to the guy that wanted to smite Walt Sidney for ruining his business?"

"That was personal," rumbled the creator of the universe.

"And this isn't?" argued his son, pointing at the television. Jim Cantore was calmly throwing various-sized fruit into an industrial garbage disposal as he explained the impending end of everything.

Amen-Ra gave a small shrug. "The planet has had a good run. And you can't tell me humanity doesn't deserve this, at least a little." He patted the armchair next to him. "Now, sit down. I feel like we don't talk anymore. How's your brother? Retired, you said? When did that happen?"

CHAPTER EIGHT
SEE YOU SPACE COWBOY

OVER THE NEXT FORTY-EIGHT HOURS, JUDY LIN AND THE SCIENTISTS at Consolidated Phukital compiled and crunched every number they could find, then rented out the newly refurbished George R. R. Martin's Rod Serling Memorial Amazon Mountain Dew Virgin Galactic Spaceport New Springsteen in southern Las Máquinas, then hauled all their crap across the country to get things set up, then set things up.

Thor Odinson, meanwhile, spent the vast majority of the time napping – or, as he preferred to call it, "saving his strength."

Eventually – after waking the thunder god up with a fire hose to the face – Thor and the rocket were prepped for launch, and the final calculations were made.

"Now, remember," explained Judy, standing behind a bank of computers in the control room and speaking into the intercom, "you need to –"

"Got it," replied Thor, his image on the monitors before the scientist.

"I feel like you should repeat it back to me, just to be sure."

"Bomb go in the hole, go boom."

"That is ... actually correct, somehow." She pulled her fingers off the intercom button. "You ever feel like maybe he's actually the smartest one of all of us?"

"No," said Queen Victoria XXX, standing behind her.

The scientist watched a sea of numbers flood her screens, graphs rising and falling, the math rearranging itself into something that meant something to her. She looked up, toward all the other scientists sitting at all the other screens across the control room. They all had their thumbs in the air.

"All right," said Judy, "here we go." She pressed the intercom again. "You ready, Thor? The countdown begins ... Now.

"10 ...
"9 ...
"8 ...
"7 ...
"6 ...
"5 ...
"4 ..."

"Wait," he said, "what if I need to –"

The Norseman's almost certainly poop-related question remained unanswered. Thor Odinson roared upward through the air, clutching the sides of the Consolidated Phukital-branded single-stage-to-orbit rocket like it was his girlfriend's waist, his flannel shirt fluttering and turning to strands as he raced to the uppermost reaches of the planet's atmosphere.

"*This is so fucking awesome!*" screamed the thunder god into the headset inside his helmet.

"There *really* should have been a better way to get him on that rocket," said Queen Victoria XXX, squinting and shaking her head a little.

"We gave him handles," explained the scientist.

"What about a spacesuit?"

"We were pressed for time," said Judy nonchalantly. "But we're not now. It's gonna take him, like, hours to get up there. Want to go get lunch?"

The queen shrugged. "Yeah, all right."

***

The dark-skinned royal replica stood at the hot bar, waiting for her mango coconut tofu bowl. She watched, with increasing curiosity, as the tiny scientist carried her plate from the salad bar to the sundae bar and began dumping heaping spoonfuls of gummi bears over her greens.

The queen raised an eyebrow.

"What?" asked the other woman, genuinely confused.

***

Judy Lin and Queen Victoria XXX watched on the monitor as a slightly roasted, free-floating – and completely nude, save for his helmet – thunder god gingerly tossed the quantum core toward the black hole, pushing himself backwards ever so slightly, his splotchy red body silhouetted against the utter darkness.

The hole, perfectly circular and perfectly pitch, was surrounded by a shimmering, ethereal gash, the interdimensional rift Thor had created years earlier when he cracked the sky. Dust and strands of barely perceptible radiation were leaking from the latter into the former, circling the black hole in dim, coruscating color.

The end result was mesmerizing, beautiful.

Thor, Queen Victoria XXX, Judy, the other scientists, they were all seeing something no woman or man – or god – had ever seen before, or ever would again.

"It looks like a vagina," said Thor.

"Oh, hey, it does," replied Judy.

The literal time bomb he had just chucked into the ether, having finally drifted close enough, began pulling and stretching toward the singularity at the center of the black hole. Several alarms started beeping in the control room.

"OK, do your thing, Thor," said the scientist, her hand on the intercom.

The Norse God of Thunder gave the camera a wink and a finger-gun, then pointed the finger toward the bomb and fired. Funneling an insane amount of electricity through himself, he charged the detonator on the device, the screens in the control room crackling and distorting as lightning danced and snapped.

The remote-controlled camera atop the rocket, furiously refocusing, panned away from the god. The bomb was glowing slightly, spikes of light still shooting out intermittently, then more and more and –

The quantum core exploded, a brilliant flash followed by an ever-expanding ball of white fire. The equipment in the control room went nuts, sensors glowing red, monitors glowing white. Then the entire system shut off and rebooted.

After a moment, the video feed came back online, flickering.

The black hole was still there.

"Why is the black hole still there?" asked Queen Victoria XXX.

Thor said something through his headset, but neither of the women could hear him. Nor could anyone else in the control room, for that matter.

Judy looked around, past scientists choking on their coffee, typing furiously, or slapping their monitors. Then, finding what she wanted, the woman without the burlap sack over her head rushed down the aisle to an empty computer station, this one linked to a camera pointed at the launch prep area.

"Crap," she said, sinking into the chair.

"What?" asked the cloned queen.

The scientist pointed toward a table in the back corner of the screen.

"What? What am I looking – Ohhh fuckballs."

Queen Victoria XXX could see that the clearly-labeled time-quickening quantum core was still sitting on the table.

She sank down in the chair next to Judy.

The two sat there solemnly for the better part of ten minutes – although, thanks to a black hole-induced time jump, it felt a lot more like thirty seconds.

"I have a *lot* of questions about how that happened," the clone eventually said, "but, first and foremost, *what the fuck did he actually explode?*"

"Best guess," said Judy, "one of the hydrogen bombs."

"Why –" She furrowed her brow. "Wouldn't that make the black hole bigger?"

"Yep."

"Fuuuuuuck," said Queen Victoria XXX, leaning into her chair so hard she nearly toppled backward.

"Pretty much."

"Wait," said the queen, bouncing forward again. "Can't we just send the *right* bomb up to him?"

"Not with a black hole *that* size, sister. Plus he's up there with our only rocket."

"So, fuck?"

"Fuck."

"Fuuuuuuuuuuuuuuck."

Meanwhile, in outer space ...

"Don't worry," Thor shouted into his headset, "I got this!"

Closing his eyes and straining every part of himself – *every* part – the Norse God of Thunder created and called lightning from the vast nothingness surrounding him, stealing energy from Earth's thermosphere, from the exosphere, siphoning signals from several satellites, changing the electromagnetic fields of Mars permanently, and even pulling what he could from the hearts of nearby stars.

A ball of electricity exploded around him, a hundred times bigger than a hundred hydrogen bombs, bigger than the blast that killed the dinosaurs. Everything went so white that calling it white was in insult to the color white.

Then it went back to being space.

Slowly, exhaustedly, the burly blonde man, floating gently in a direction he couldn't quite pin down, opened his eyes.

The massive black void had only gotten even more massive and voidier, a twisting rope of Smurf blue swirling around the edges now, all that was left of the interdimensional rift that the singularity had swallowed wholesale.

"That's probably not good."

A chunk of space debris whizzed by Thor's head, part of a satellite he had inadvertently blown up, followed by a few more slabs of interstellar shrapnel. The Consolidated Phukital rocket, his return ride, was nowhere to be seen, either exploded or eaten by the black hole. The thunder god's amiable backwards drift, meanwhile, stopped being backwards and stopped being so amiable. He could feel his leg hairs being yanked out one by one, his regular hairs, his beard, being pulled forward toward the singularity.

"I, uh, I think I want to come home now," he said, a little frantically.

There was no response.

"Hello?" He tapped his helmet.

"Anyone?"

CHAPTER NINE
SUPERUNKNOWN

THOR ODINSON, NORSE GOD OF THUNDER, MIGHTIEST OF THE AESIR and sworn protector of Asgard, was not one for introspection. His existence consisted almost exclusively of fighting and fucking and discovering brand new levels of intoxication. Deep thinking and the contemplation of the self were so far from his wheelhouse that he'd need a map to find them – and he wasn't exactly one for maps either. But, now, floating impotently through space, hundreds of miles from his friends, from food and porn and all his stuff, inching inexorably closer to a superpowered black hole, the naked god suddenly found himself introspecting like a motherfucker.

Well, he thought, *shit.*

I guess this is it. I guess this is how I'm going out: Swallowed by a hole in the universe – and not the good kind of swallowed or the good kind of hole. Not bleeding out after slaying Jörmungandr, not punching that stupid sea serpent in his stupid face and bringing on Ragnarok and taking everyone else with me. Not in a blaze of glory on the lava fields of Múspellsheimr; not in Asgard; not in Vanaheimr or Niflheimr, but fucking Midgard, lamest of the Nine Worlds. And not even on frigging Midgard, but in the infinite ball of nothing surrounding it.

I mean, who does that? Who layers their sky like a frigging Jell-O cake? Atmosphere, smatmosphere. Either have air or don't, make up your mind.

The thunder god could feel himself turning, could feel his scrotum being tugged, and ungently at that.

I should've known this was going to happen, he thought.

Well, not this, *specifically*, he continued thinking, *obviously. But, you know, something equally as stupid and pointless.*

From the second I crashed into that idiot swamp, I should've known that I was doomed. No powers, none, and the first guy I meet is a donut maker, the first guy I meet in a reality where I can get fat is fucking Ali, a guy who makes tiny frosted rings of fried fucking dough for a living. And then pancakes and regular cakes and then I get a job where all I do is sit on my ass eating delicious, delicious crap and taking orders from some half-robot and listening to fucking customers whine about their fucking pillows.

Honestly, If I hadn't 've already visited Hel, I woulda said this was it.

But the worst part? The craziest part?

Somewhere along the way, I started caring.

About Catrina and Ali, about Charlie and Vicky and Timmy and Bo, and even Mark and Billy sometimes.

That's where I really fucked up.

Thor rotated around, could see the Earth clearly before him: blue and green and brown and scarred almost beyond recognition. But still there, still spinning. Still teeming with life, that life teeming with other life, all of it, all the way down, fighting to keep on living. Fucking, to keep on existing. And discovering brand new ways of getting intoxicated to do the other two things.

I'm not supposed to love this stupid fucking planet.

This isn't supposed to be my home.

I'm not supposed to care about the people on it, not supposed to want to help them.

But it is and I do and everything is fucked. Because of me. Because I tried to help.

Me. Thor, Odin's Son, God of Motherfucking Thunder.

What the fuck good have I actually done?

What the fuck good is a god that can't save the people he loves?

The glass of the thunder god's helmet cracked like a rupturing fault line, the near-vacuum of lower space sucking out the oxygen.

Great, he thought, *and now my face is cold.*

Fuck.

Fuuuck.

Maybe this is how it's supposed to end.

Maybe this is how it needs *to end.*

The Norseman rotated again, the Earth before him again. His own face was reflected back at him on the helmet's cracked glass.

And maybe I'm all right with that?

A sense of peace washed over the thunder god, a strange calming presence he couldn't ever remember feeling before. His body relaxed. He could feel the gravity of the black hole beckoning to him, could feel himself drifting inevitably closer.

Then Thor farted.

The average fart exits the average butthole at approximately one meter per second, which, according to Newtonian law, should propel the average human forward, at least a little. Factor in pants, decency, and Earth's gravity, however, and that momentum is, for all intents and purposes, negated.

Even with gravity and proper interstellar outerwear removed from the equation – and there is one, look it up – the average astronaut would need several *lifetimes* to fart themselves up to a decent speed.

But Thor was no average astronaut.

And neither was his butthole.

The thunder god angled his anus as best he could, farting his way through the galaxy's grossest K-turn and maneuvering himself, his trajectory, toward the planet Earth. Then, the massive orb floating directly over his head, the Norse God of Thunder thundered forward, passing gas through his ass in fat blasts as fast as he could amass them.

With each fart, the planet before him grew bigger and bigger. Flexing his insides, crimping and contracting, Thor eked out every last gasp of colonic wind within him, soaring through the stars on his own flatulence, increasingly desperate for gravity to grab hold of him and take him home.

And then it did.

Hard.

"Fuuuuuuuuuuuuuuuuuuuuuuuuuuuuuuuuuuuuuuuuuuuuuuuuuuuuu uuuuuuuuuuuuuuuuuuuuuuuuuuuuuuuuuuuuuuuuuuuuuuuuuuuuuuuuuu uuuuuuuuuuuuuuuuuuuuuccccccccccccccccccccccccccccccccccccccc–"

Thor Odinson landed face-first in the middle of the Las Máquinas desert, hitting the ground at well over the speed of sound.

"Isn't this ... supposed to happen in water?" he asked, pulling himself out of the second massive hole he'd created that day. Resting with his arms over the rim, the dust slowly settling around him, the burly, bearded blonde man could see Queen Victoria XXX and Judy Lin hopping from a Consolidated Phukital van and rushing toward him.

"Any luck?" asked the queen, grabbing his hand and pulling him to ground. "What's going on up there?"

"We lost all of our equipment," added Judy.

"Yeah, it's, uh, it's bad," explained Thor. "Like, real bad."

"How big is the hole?"

"Big," the Norseman explained flatly. The lack of a "your mom" joke spoke volumes.

Queen Victoria XXX wobbled a little, then slumped to the ground.

"What now?" she asked, her voice empty.

"I ... I don't know," said Judy, shaking her head. "If we knew more about what kind of bomb the penguins built, maybe ..." She shrugged her shoulders weakly.

"I'm fine, by the way," said Thor, clearing the dirt and dust from his charred skin.

"OK, but ... how?" asked the queen, continuing to ignore her friend.

"I've got an idea," said the scientist.

CHAPTER TEN

I WANTED TO CALL IT THE DICK CHENEY MEMORIAL INTERROGATION ROOM, BUT I ALREADY USED THAT JOKE FOR SATAN'S CONFERENCE ROOM BACK IN HIGH VOLTAGE

JUDY LIN EXITED THE INTERROGATION ROOM COVERED IN BLOOD and tiny black feathers.

"Well?" asked Queen Victoria XXX.

"Wrong colors," said the scientist, "different faction."

"Huh," replied the clone. "I want to be surprised that there's competing penguin terrorist groups, but, honestly, I'm just not."

CHAPTER TEN, TAKE TWO

THEN I THOUGHT, THERE'S NO REASON WHY MULTIPLE THINGS COULDN'T BE NAMED AFTER THE SAME PERSON
I MEAN, LOOK AT WASHINGTON AND JEFFERSON

JUDY LIN EXITED THE INTERROGATION ROOM COVERED IN BLOOD and tiny black feathers.

"Better luck this time?" asked Queen Victoria XXX.

"Not for *anyone* involved."

CHAPTER TEN, TAKE THREE

OF COURSE, THEN I'D BE COMPARING DICK CHENEY TO GEORGE WASHINGTON AND THOMAS JEFFERSON, AND, WELL, THAT DIDN'T SEEM RIGHT

JUDY LIN EXITED THE INTERROGATION ROOM COVERED IN BLOOD and tiny black feathers.

"Well?"

"Apparently this guy's colors are more cerulean, and we're looking for more of a powder blue."

"Sif's steely snatch," grumbled the queen.

CHAPTER TEN, TAKE FOUR

I MEAN, THEY ALL HAD THEIR FAULTS, AND, OBVIOUSLY, SOME VERRRY SIMILAR — AND HIGHLY PROBLEMATIC — ISSUES WHEN IT CAME TO RESPECTING THE SANCTITY AND VALUE OF HUMAN LIFE

JUDY LIN EXITED THE INTERROGATION ROOM COVERED IN BLOOD and tiny black feathers.

Queen Victoria XXX raised an eyebrow.

The scientist shook her head.

CHAPTER TEN, TAKE FIVE

BUT AT LEAST THE FOUNDING FATHERS TALKED A GOOD GAME, AND DID SOME DECENT THINGS

JUDY LIN EXITED THE INTERROGATION ROOM COVERED IN BLOOD and tiny black feathers.

"There's a beak in your hair," said Queen Victoria XXX, pointing without uncrossing her arms.

CHAPTER TEN, TAKE SIX
RIGHT?

JUDY LIN EXITED THE INTERROGATION ROOM COVERED IN BLOOD and tiny black feathers.

"I don't think that one was even a penguin," she said.

CHAPTER TEN, TAKE SEVEN

LOOK, I, UH, I GOT A LITTLE OFF TRACK HERE

JUDY LIN EXITED THE INTERROGATION ROOM COVERED IN BLOOD and tiny black feathers.

"Are you planning on taking a shower at any point?" asked Queen Victoria XXX. She crinkled her nose. "You're starting to smell."

CHAPTER TEN, TAKE EIGHT

AMERICA?

JUDY LIN EXITED THE INTERROGATION ROOM COVERED IN BLOOD and tiny black feathers.

"OK, how about this time?" asked the queen.

"Well, she's definitely the right terrorist organization."

"Fucking *finally*," she replied. "So, what did she have to say?"

"Honestly, it's pretty hard to hear anything over the screaming."

Queen Victoria XXX bit her lip and stared at the scientist. Then: "You know, I don't even have a *soul* and this seems *really* wrong."

"Yeah," replied Judy, shaking gore from her hands. "The penguins aren't big fans either."

CHAPTER ELEVEN
FAST-FORWARD

"ANY LUCK TALKING TO DAD?" ASKED THOR ODINSON, CELL phone on speaker as he sat on the curb outside Consolidated Phukital's secret black ops torture facility.

"No such luck, brother," said Jesus Christ.

"Well, that's a bummer."

"You're telling me."

A moment. Then Thor asked: "Wanna meet us for lunch?"

"Yeah, all right," said the Prince of Peace. "Where –"

The god and the Son of God were at a diner, narrow and comfy, sitting down in a large booth overlooking the industrial parks of New West Ninth Street Northeast.

"How about here?" said Thor.

"Uh, yeah, OK, here's –"

In less than the blink of an eye, the deific duo was joined by Queen Victoria XXX, Judy Lin, Artemis Agroterê, and Catherine the Great LXIX, all of them crowded into the same booth.

"You're seeing this too, right?" asked Jesus. Then, mumbling, he added: "I really shouldn't have smoked earlier."

"When did you guys get here?" asked Thor.

"When *did* we get here?" echoed Queen Victoria XXX, looking around.

"And why are there dinosaurs outside?" asked Artemis, Greek Goddess of the Hunt, pointing her chin toward the window.

There were, indeed, dinosaurs outside. A pack of diplodocus diplodichied past the diner, the building rumbling as the massive beasts trudged slowly by, silverware rattling and waters spilling. A pair of eagle-sized rhamphorhynchus sailed over them, leathery wings spread, their throat pouches full and wriggling with their next meals.

There was also, it should be noted, a decided lack of city surrounding the rambling reptiles.

"Are we in Cretaceous Park?" asked Jesus.

"Nope," said Judy, pulling up the map on her phone, "West New New York."

"So, did they get loose from a carnival," asked Catherine the Great LXIX, "or ..."

The diplodocus honked and scattered, stumbling and stampeding away as a ceratosaurus appeared next to the booth, just outside the window. The eight-foot-tall theropod lumbered forward, baring a mouth full of teeth like ceramic steak knives.

"My guess," explained the scientist, "the diner just blinked back to the Jurassic era. Or the Jurassic era jumped around the diner. Either way, the black hole is clearly *completely* wrecking the space-time continuum right now."

"Oh, man," said Jesus, "this is gonna get a whole lot crazier, isn't it?"

"Almost certain—"

"—ly!" Catherine the Great LXIX was shouting, slamming her mechanical fist against the table and lifting her Rubenesque frame from her seat. "We can't just bend over and take it!"

"I don't think any of us were suggesting that?" said Artemis, hands raised, steadying herself and unsure of a lot of things.

"I might have been?" conceded Thor.

"OK, but, for real? Or as a dirty joke?" asked Queen Victoria XXX.

The blonde man shrugged. "Kinda fifty-fifty there."

"Maybe we should try to time how long it is in between jumps," said Artemis, the lithe archer pulling a stopwatch from her antique leather satchel. "See if maybe there's some kind of rhyme or reas—"

"— son!" shouted Thor. "Whoa, that was —"

"— balls," said Queen Victoria XXX. "I mean, who doesn't —"

"— shower?" said Judy, looking down at her remarkably unpenguinified clothes. "When did that happen? Did anyone see me —"

"— take a dump," said Catherine the Great LXIX, scooching out of the booth. "Wait, I don't have to poop. I — No, wait, I have to poop." The cloned empress rushed toward the rear of the restaurant.

"Is it already three o'clock?" asked Artemis, looking at her phone.

"You know when she poops?" asked Queen Victoria XXX.

"Of course," replied the Greek goddess. "You live with someone long enough, you notice these things. Are you telling me you don't know when Thor —"

"– masturbates?" she concluded. "OK, even I don't know what that one was."

Everyone at the table looked at everyone else at the table, frozen, waiting for the next time jump and desperately not wanting to be the one who said "masturbates" for seemingly no reason.

They waited.

They waited some more.

Thor scratched his knee.

Jesus sipped his coffee.

They waited some more.

"Huh," said Queen Victoria XXX.

"So much for that theory," said Jesus.

Out of nowhere, Catherine the Great LXIX reappeared in the booth.

"I hope you washed your hands," said Artemis.

"You and me both," said the replicated Russian royal.

"Fuck it. Fuck this," said Queen Victoria XXX, shaking her dark, wild head of hair. "I assume we're all here to compare notes, right? Then let's do it, let's just –"

An empty plate of mozzarella sticks appeared in the center of the table. The dinosaurs outside had been replaced by sea monsters and giant squids, while the air had been replaced by murky water. The diner, thankfully, appeared to be fortified, pressurized, and rated for underwater occupation.

"God damn it!" yelled the queen, showering crumbs across the table.

"Which –" began Thor.

"Motherfucker!" concluded Thor, pulling a fork from his neck.

"Does anyone remember what we were talking about?" asked the clone. "Where we ended up, strategy-wise?"

"I seem to recall unrelenting doom," said Artemis.

"Sounds right to me, sister," seconded Jesus.

"That can't be –"

"– right?"

"What other options do we –"

"– have?" asked the waitress, standing impatiently at the table's edge.

"Eggs."

"Bacon."

"Pan–"

"– cakes? How would that even –"

"– work? Nah, I've just been –"

"– sick," mumbled Catherine the Great LXIX, looking a little green. "'scuse me." She rushed to the bathroom once again.

Artemis grabbed the arm of a passing waiter.

"Have you guys been jumping through time haphazardly? Like, more than normal?"

"Thank you," she said, letting go of him. Turning toward the rest of the table, she explained: "He said it hasn't actually been that bad for them, other than the dinosaurs and fish monsters."

"Then what the shit?" asked Queen Victoria XXX. "Why are all the time jumps seemingly concentrated right here, at this table?"

"Maybe the table's magic, man," offered Jesus Christ.

"Or maybe it's 'cause Jesus, Artemis, and me exist out of time, more or less?" answered Thor. "And we're, you know, super-powered? Plus, I went to space."

"So did I," said Catherine the Great LXIX, reappearing at the table. "Remember?"

"No," answered the thunder god. "But, still. There we go. Maybe we're, like, absorbing more of the space raviolis, or whatever they are. Space spaghetti?"

Judy Lin furrowed her brow. "Most of that was make-believe nonsense," she scolded, "and the rest of it was pasta." Then the scientist reversed both her eyebrows and her stance on the subject. "But, given what we're dealing with –" She shrugged. "– sure. Why the hell not."

The waitress arrived with their food.

The food was gone.

"I don't like any part of this," rumbled Thor.

The scenery outside of the window returned to that of a city. But not the city the sixsome was actually in. Well, OK, technically, it *was* the correct *city*, but not the correct *time*. The gods, the demigod, the clones, and the scientist were now sitting in Secaucus, New Jersey, five years earlier, before most of northern New Jersey was annexed by New New York, D.C. and relabeled as West New New York.

A redheaded woman in a plaid miniskirt and a Sex Pistols t-shirt walked past the window. A very familiar-looking redheaded woman.

"Bo!" gasped Thor and Queen Victoria XXX, simultaneously.

"You guys know h–"

They were already gone.

CHAPTER TWELVE
ONCE UPON A TIME

BOUDICA IX, CLONE OF THE FIRST CENTURY CELTIC WARRIOR QUEEN, friend of Queen Victoria XXX, and former girlfriend of Thor Odinson, was supposed to be dead. She had been impaled by an orc two years earlier while defending the city-state of Las Vegas from an onslaught of murderous monsters, devastating the aforementioned heroes, as well as straight-up ruining her then-husband, the current Benevolent Dictator of FARTSSS, William H. Taft XLII.

As one might imagine, seeing her alive again, wandering aimlessly through the streets and blissfully unaware of her impending tragedy, was kind of a kick in the nuts.

"Bo!" shouted Thor, racing after her. "Bo!"

The cloned queen turned. "Yes?" she asked, cocking an eyebrow.

"It's me!"

"Mario? You don't look like an Italian plumber."

"No, I'm ... I'm Thor, Norse God of –"

"That's a weird name."

"No, Bo, it's me, *Thor*. Honeyballs. Sugarpubes. We ... We ..."

"There's a bathroom in the Starbucks around the corner, weirdo."

"I don't – What? No, you and me, we were – we're going to get together."

"I kinda doubt that, buddy. You are waaay too jacked for my tastes."

"Boudica!" called Queen Victoria XXX, rushing up behind the beefy Norseman.

"Vicky?" asked the redhead, tilting her head around the thunder god's shoulder.

"Hi."

"Hi," replied Boudica IX. "What're you doing here? You know this guy?"

"It's a ..." She grimaced. "It's a long story."

"Is this because of Andy? Because, look, I didn't know you two were a thing. And, in my defense, I didn't really care either."

"No, it's not ... It's just ... It's really good to see you again."

"Yeah," echoed Thor.

"Uh, OK?" replied the redheaded woman. "Nice to see you too?"

"You don't sound sure about that," said the queen.

"Well, we kinda don't have a great history ..."

"What are you –" said Queen Victoria XXX. "Oh. Ohhh. Right."

"Yeah."

"'cause of the –"

"Yeah."

"With the –"

"Yeah."

"Right," said the dark-haired queen, "sorry about that."

The other queen shrugged. "No skin off my butt."

"Actually there was a *lot* of skin off your butt."

"Is that what that was?" asked Thor. "I thought maybe you went down a slide too fast or –"

"*What?*" roared Boudica IX. "How in the farts do –"

"Oh, OK, that makes sense," finished the queen.

"Wait, for reals?" asked Queen Victoria XXX. "The black hole, the time jumps ... *Thor* explained that? Adequately?"

"Sure," said Boudica IX, shrugging. "Space is weird."

"Huh." The other queen bit her lip. "OK, look, I don't know if I'm supposed to tell you this or not," explained the Hanoverian homunculus, "but you're going to get stabbed in the chest by an orc while fighting a cave troll in Las Vegas, so ... maybe don't do that. If you can help it."

"Also," added Thor, "Vicky's going to murder you in a porn warehouse, but that's kind of how you and I get together and, I don't know –" He cleared his throat. "– I know it all fell apart but we ... we had a lot of fun while it lasted, so ... your call on whether or not you want to not die that time too."

"OK, hold on, that's ... that's kind of a lot," said Boudica IX, pulling out her phone and pulling up the Notepad app. "I die twice?"

"Yeah, but we're going to used to know a guy who could fix that."

"Up until he dies too," added Queen Victoria XXX.

"Suuuper violently," added the god.

"OK ..." said the Celtic clone, scrunching her face. "Can you be more specific, though? Are there, you know, dates for any of this? 'cause I already have a *bunch* of feuds with, like, a dozen clans of cave tr–"

The cityscape shifted again.

Boudica IX was gone.

Queen Victoria XXX and Thor Odinson were alone on the sidewalk. In the distance, the grey-green sky was stretching and spiraling, being pulled into the increasingly visible black hole like filthy, slow-moving toilet water.

"I wish that stupid fucking hole would just get things over with already," grumbled the thunder god, glaring up. He began stomping back towards the diner, buildings rattling as he passed.

"I don't," quietly replied the clone.

CHAPTER THIRTEEN
(DO THE) MASHED POTATOES

THOR ODINSON ENTERED THE DINER AND FOUND HIS FRIENDS right where he'd left them. As the door shut behind him, reality shuddered. Judy Lin was suddenly wearing a bag over her head again.

"Are you fucking ..." The woman wriggled beneath the burlap sack, trying to settle the eye holes. "Right," she said, putting her hands on the table. "I'm out."

"Good," said the thunder god. "Let's –"

He was sitting at the table again.

"This is the opposite of what I wanted to do."

"Are we *sure* this diner isn't haunted, man?" asked Jesus Christ.

"Honestly, anything's an option at this point," said Judy.

"Yeah?" said Artemis Agroterê. "Then there has to be *something* we can do to –"

Everyone was suddenly covered – *covered* – in mashed potatoes.

"There we go, apparently," said the woman with the bag over her head.

"Uh ..." inquired the Greek goddess, looking at her potato-plastered hands.

"I second that 'uh ...'" seconded Catherine the Great LXIX, doing the same.

"I'm kind of surprised we didn't do this earlier," replied Judy.

"What?"

"You guys don't know?"

"Don't know what?" asked Jesus.

"Potatoes are space-time anomalies, existing outside of the generally accepted continuum," explained the scientist, flinging smashed spuds as she gesticulated. "They operate under their own rules. That's how come you can pull them from the ground and they keep growing."

"So ..." asked Thor, "why are we wearing them?"

"To ... block the space raviolis?" offered Judy.

"You're kidding me," said Artemis.

The scientist shrugged noncommittally.

"*None of this makes any fucking sense!*"

"Now you're getting it."

"Here's the check," said the skinny blonde waitress, sliding the bill onto the table. "Whenever you're ready."

"Holy shit," said Jesus Christ, his eyes going wide as he picked up the tray. "Were these potatoes made out of gold or something?"

"You've been here for, like, twelve hours. The big guy had, I dunno, four meals?"

"Well, in that case," began Thor, heaving himself up from the booth, "anyone up for a dine-and-dash?"

"Guys," said the waitress, "I'm still right –"

She was suddenly alone.

"Where'd they go?" She looked out the window, at the early Colonial Era pastoral scene before her. "And why am I even still working? Nadia, you've got to learn to *prioritize*."

CHAPTER FOURTEEN

THE DICE WAS LOADED FROM THE START

QUEEN VICTORIA XXX WAS WALKING AIMLESSLY DOWN THE STREET, hands tight in the pockets of her hoodie, kicking an empty soda can, and then a rock, and then, accidentally, a small lizard, as reality held a fashion show around her.

"Sorry!" she called after the lizard, the scaly green iguana-thing rolling end over end.

The lizard turned into a cannonball and came to rest in an open field.

The raven-haired royal replica suddenly found herself in the middle of the Revolutionary War. American forces marched past her, on their way to what used to be – and was again, apparently – Jersey City, and the Battle of Paulus Hook. Guns roared dully in the distance; plumes of smoke rose from the horizon.

This, thought the clone, *is bullshit.*

But it's better than nothing, I guess.

And nothing's all I got coming for me.

Fighting back tears, the cloned queen looked for somewhere to sit, then gave up and plopped down onto the grass, watching the soldiers soldier down the dirt road.

It must be nice, she thought, *having a soul. Having something to look forward to after you die. Even if you're wrong. At least you've got that hope to get you through.*

But what have I got?

I was created – created – from crumbling bones and leftover spit and science-magic. To be a politician, cutthroat and cold, with no one else's interests in mind but mine. To be an assassin, violent and efficient, to take orders without a thought, to kill on command. To be a celebrity, to make women want me and men want to be me.

I was created with someone else's life inside of mine.

And, yeah, I've played the roles, gone along for the ride, sometimes willingly, sometimes without even knowing. But they're not me.

Not really.

Not entirely.

I've been a mercenary and a stoner and a housewife. I've punched and I've screwed and I've screamed and I've cried and I've loved and I've lost and I've saved the friggin' world and I've done nothing at all and I still ...

I still don't know who I am, not really.

I never bothered to figure that out, did I?

I was so tangled up with my programming, with Charlie, and then ... Then I just kind of gave up, took some time to figure things out.

Time.

I always thought I'd have more time.

The queen looked up at the sky, at the clouds churning towards oblivion.

But I don't get that, do I?

She raised a middle finger, long and hard and proud.

Eat a dick, universe.

Reality shimmered. Queen Victoria XXX was in Secaucus again, sitting on a bus stop bench. Nine years earlier. (Or two-hundred-and-fifty-nine years *later*, depending on which way you're doing the math.)

"Great," she grumbled at the black hole, "now when the –"

Her eyes went wide.

In front of her was *her*: Queen Victoria XXX, shortly after being released from the Aussichtslos Drogensucht Gesellschaft mit beschränkter Haftung survivor dorms, shortly after murdering all the other Victorian clones. Green – and a little red and purple, from the brawling – and on her own for the first time. Still in a vintage long coat, velvet and lace everywhere, her hair immaculate.

"– fuck."

"God damn it," said the Queen Victoria XXX from the past. She grabbed the closest parking meter with both hands, started wrenching it free from the sidewalk. "I thought I took care of all of you."

"No, I'm not ..." The queen not trying to murder herself put up her hands. "I'm not another clone, I'm ... I'm you – actual *you* – from the future."

"What?"

Current Queen Victoria XXX pointed a finger toward the sky, toward the roiling, electric blue hole inexorably undoing the entirety of existence.

"I don't understand what that has to do with anything," said the other one.

"It's a ... Shit, you haven't seen a time anomaly yet. And Charlie hasn't made you take a beginner astrophysics course at the community college."

"Charlie? Who the fuck is Charlie?"

"All right, look." The slightly older dark-skinned monarch lifted up the edge of her t-shirt, showed off the minefield of tiny, faded scars across her stomach. "Remember? When Susan B. Anthony III ambushed us? I bet that was last week for you."

The younger clone absently put a hand to her abdomen. "How ..."

"I told you, I'm you."

"Yeah, no, but seriously: how?"

"Space is weird?"

"OK," said the previous version of the political impersonation, shaking her head. "OK, all right, but, even if that's true ... Then, what?"

"I, uh, I don't know. I wasn't exactly *planning* this."

The Queen Victoria XXX from ten years earlier, not yet raging against her programming, still unsusceptible to existential crises, simply shrugged.

"OK. Then I'm just gonna –"

"No," said the more reasonable clone, "don't ..."

"Why not?"

"I ... *I don't know.* I just feel like I should ..."

"What? Give me some advice? How badly did you screw up our life?"

"No, it's not – It's not that," she said. "Well, maybe ..."

"Super helpful, lady."

"Look, just ... don't ... don't do what I did," she said. "Because we know how that turns out, and ... and it hurts. And then it's over. So, try something different, *anything* different. Kiss that girl at the bar. That dog you adopt? He's actually a bomb. Brussels sprouts aren't anywhere as terrible as you think, stop leaving your iPod in the car, and, if you and Thor end up fighting a terrorist penguin cell, don't let him throw the black hole generator into an interdimensional tear in the sky."

Queen Victoria XXX, the one from the past, raised an eyebrow.

Queen Victoria XXX, the current one, wrinkled hers.

"And don't ... don't fall in love with Charlie, with Chester A. Arthur XVII," she continued. "I mean, maybe it's worth it, but, honestly, right now, I'm ... I'm not sure. I don't have anything to compare it against.

"Or *do* fall in love with him," she continued, "but don't let him die. And, I mean, that's gonna be hard because he dies aaalll the time."

"Chester A. Arthur XVII? The boy scout-y nerd?"

"He's going to be the best thing that ever happened to you."

"I find that hard to believe."

"Then don't."

"Man," said the younger Queen Victoria XXX, leaning an elbow on the parking meter, "you are *seriously* bumming me out right now, me. I kinda figured we'd just, you know, make out or something, but, Jesus Christ."

"We actually don't use 'Jesus Christ' as a swear anymore," explained the other clone. "Turns out he's a good dude. He sells us our weed. Well, gives. I honestly don't remember the last time we paid him."

"Wait, we're on drugs in the future? What the hell kind of –"

But Queen Victoria XXX was gone again.

Secaucus was West New New York again.

Queen Victoria XXX was alone again.

"I really miss not feeling feelings," she mumbled, curling up on top of the bench.

A few minutes later and half a block away, Judy Lin, Jesus Christ and Thor Odinson turned a corner. Seeing the queen, the blonde man jogged closer.

"There you are," said the Norseman. "Are you – What's wrong?"

"I can't fucking take this anymore," growled the queen, getting up and squeezing him and resting her head on his shoulder.

The thunder god put his arms around her, gently.

"That sounds like a cue to get blackout drunk."

"That sounds amazing," she said, sniffling. Then: "Why are you covered in mashed potatoes?"

CHAPTER FIFTEEN

[INSERT .GIF OF FUTURAMA'S BENDER GOING "DOOOOOOOOOOOOOOOOOOMMMEEEDDD!"]

THERE HAD BEEN TWENTY-SEVEN-AND-A-HALF APOCALYPSES TO DATE. People had survived so much, so many times, they thought they could survive anything.

The Antarctic supercolliders the planet had used to shift the planet's orbit decades earlier, to avoid an asteroid, the ones that had rocked the planet so hard they ended up ending the world for the second time all on their own, were dusted off and turned on.

Other scientists with other time-quickening quantum cores strapped other gods to other rockets, tried every other thing they could think of. Bombs and theoretical isotopes and busses full of experimental monkeys were tossed into the black hole; artificial supernovas, all of Earth's potatoes, and anything that sucked real hard, like industrial vacuums and Seth McFarlane's exhumed corpse. A few industrious Swiss engineers even managed to create a new black hole inside the first one, acting under the premise that they'd simply cancel one another out.

They did not.

Nothing, in fact, did anything.

In a desperate Hail Mary, a distress beacon was hurled into space – on the opposite side of the planet from the black hole, obviously – the hope being that maybe some heretofore unknown alien race was looking for a new species to adopt or enslave.

The black hole, meanwhile, kept getting bigger.

The Earth kept being doomed.

CHAPTER SIXTEEN

LIKE IT'S 1999

"SO," ASKED QUEEN VICTORIA XXX, SHOUTING OVER THE DIN OF the bar, "we're sure we're fucked, right?"

"Incontrovertibly," answered Judy Lin, once more bag free.

"I don't know what that means," said Thor Odinson.

"Like, completely and totally, brother," said Jesus Christ.

"OK."

"And there's no chance that past me might get her shit together and save us all?" asked the cloned queen, crowding closer to her friends. The tavern was packed tighter than a tin of polyamorous sardines prone to orgies and into anal play.

"Probably not," explained the scientist. "All the instances of the past appearing are, as near as I can tell, more like visions than actionable moments of our reality. Maybe there's some alternate timeline where we don't all die horribly, but not the one we're in. I mean, you don't have a memory of telling yourself stuff, right?"

"Oh. Uh, no."

"Then there you go." Judy paused, then shouted: "Hey, can I keep hanging out with you guys? I feel like you'd really know how to have a good time."

"Sure," replied the clone, shrugging. "But before we get started –" Queen Victoria XXX pulled a folded-up liability waiver from the back pocket of her jeans. "– we're legally required to have you sign this."

"For real?"

"When we go on a tear," she explained, "we go on a motherfucking tear. And I'm gonna tear this tear a new one."

"Yeah, but, the doom, remember?"

"Look," said Thor, "we don't want you or your family suing us for damages or wrongful death or whatever in the meantime and ruining our last couple of days."

"Fair enough," replied the scientist, pulling a pen from her coat pocket.

"So does this mean you guys are cashing out?" asked Abraham Lincoln XVI, leaning closer to the trio.

"For real, man?" asked the thunder god.

"What?" replied the bartender. The last of the surviving Lincolns, Abraham Lincoln XVI was a lanky, gnarled leather tree of a man, the result of some questionable genetics and an increasingly unfair life.[v] "Weren't you the ones going on about not wanting your last days ruined?"

"Yeah," said Thor, "but we were talking about *us*."

"Abe," added Queen Victoria XXX, "what in our entire history makes you think that we're going to pay you right now?"

"Or that we even have that kind of money," added the thunder god.

There was a glint in the dead president's good eye. "I was really hoping you were gonna say that." He began rolling up his sleeves.

"If this is going to get violent, man, then I'm outta here," said Jesus Christ.

"Hot damn," said Thor, draining his beer mug and then smashing it against the bar top. "Now it's a fucking party."

Abraham Lincoln XVI punched him in the face.

Judy Lin threw a tumbler at the president's head. Queen Victoria XXX tackled the scientist to the floor. Thor grabbed her stool and hurled it across the room. Abraham Lincoln XVI smashed a whiskey bottle over the god's head.

Then a man in the back said "Everyone attack!" and it turned into a barroom blitz.

It was electric.

So frantically hectic.

It was like lightning.

Everybody was fighting.

So then someone put Sweet's "Ballroom Blitz" on the jukebox and everybody started hitting everybody else in perfect time with the song.

"Right," said the Prince of Peace, putting down the rest of his Scotch. A plate and a half-eaten hamburger sailed over his shoulder. "I'm outta here."

***

Flames were rising from the collapsed frame of Honest Abe's Taphouse, stained glass windows bubbling and popping. As thick smoke twisted into the air, a few stragglers could still be seen crawling out from the wreckage, bruised and scratched and bleeding, while dozens of other patrons were on the sidewalk, pouring one out for their homies.

"So," asked Abraham Lincoln XVI, wiping blood from his face, "where to next?"

"We're going dancing," said Queen Victoria XXX.

***

Barefoot, sweating, her jacket somewhere else, Queen Victoria XXX danced like no one was watching.

Then she danced like everyone was watching.

She was, quite literally, a dancing queen.

She busted a move.

Her hips didn't lie.

She shaked her groove thing.

She shaked her bon-bon.

She shake, shake, shaked her booty.

There was a whole lotta shakin' goin' on.

She danced with the one that brought her.

She danced with somebody.

She was dancing with herself.

She shut up and danced.

She just danced.

Ella bailó.

She turned the beat around.

She danced like the rhythm was gonna get her.

She danced until there was blood on the dance floor.

She danced until there was a murder on the dance floor. DJ, she was gonna burn this God damned house right down.

She was a maniac, a maniac.

The police were called, but no one answered.

The music was killed, the lights were shut off.

The roof, the roof was on fire.

But Queen Victoria XXX kept dancing, dancing in the dark.

The groove was in her heart.

She was dancing on the ceiling, as it fell down around her.

She was dancing in the street.

She was dancing in the moonlight.

Thor grabbed her by the shoulder.

Flames were rising from the collapsed frame of the Warehouse dance club, cement toppling inwards, rebar jutting into the night, all of it lit up purple and red and blue by a handful of strobe lights still flashing inside.

"Oh. Well, that got out of hand," said Queen Victoria XXX, breathing heavily, wiping someone else's blood from her face. "Where to next?"

"I think I know a place," said Thor.

***

"Thor!" shouted the Neo-Vikings at the bar, raising their glasses.

"Sorry about that," said the thunder god to his friends, in a not unsubtle humblebrag, "I'm kind of a —"

"Vicky!" roared the entire tavern, cheering. "Huzzah!" Steins clanked together.

"Mine's bigger," said the queen.

***

The Norse God of Thunder threw open the door to the "men's room," otherwise known as a filthy back alley that was only hosed down once a week, unless it rained.

He found Judy Lin squatting in the corner, pants around her knees, holding onto the chain-link fence for support.

"What?" she asked.

"There's an actual ladies' room in there," said Thor, pointing with his thumb, "with plumbing and everything."

"There was a line," she explained with a small shrug, "and those Viking women ..."

"Good point," said the thunder god, settling in a respectable distance away and undoing his fly. "I actually had a thing with a Viking woman once. Man, could she wreck up an outhouse."

"You're kidding."

"No, I'm serious. Back in the day ..."

***

Thor Odinson pulled open the door to the bar and found himself in the mid-1800s.

"This isn't McSorley's," he grumbled. "Is it?"

"Oy, boyo," shouted the grizzled bartender. "No women allowed. Git yer vazey tarts on outta here."

"What did you just call us?" roared Queen Victoria XXX.

Several patrons – large, snaggletoothed, and presumably part of at least one of the then-flourishing Irish mobs – stood up slowly from their tables and barstools.

"Ya got 'til the count o' three," said the barkeep, "unless ya be wantin' trouble."

"Trouble?" repeated the thunder god, cocking an eyebrow.

"Gentlemen," said Abraham Lincoln XVI, stepping to the front. He smiled. "We would like nothing more."

***

Flames were rising from the collapsed frame of McSorley's Ale House.

"Maybe if we wait a while, we'll transport back a few more years and we can burn it down again," said Thor, picking snaggled teeth out of his knuckles.

***

The cloned queen climbed on top of the thunder god, her mouth all over his. She started pulling at the buttons on his shirt.

"Yes!" shouted the scientist, twisting in the passenger seat to get a better look. "I knew it!"

Queen Victoria XXX threw her shoe at her.

"Guys," said Abraham Lincoln XVI, looking into the rearview mirror. "Come on."

Thor threw his shoe at him.

The car swerved across two lanes before righting itself again.

"That was a *boot*, man," grumbled the president. "Not cool."

***

"Yeah, give me four Death in the Afternoons." The clone turned toward her friends. "What do you guys want?"

***

"Hang on, guysh," slurred Judy Lin, wobbling toward a coffee vending machine. "I just wanna ..." She fell hard against the machine, leaning on it with her shoulder as she fished around in her pocket for change.

Finding a couple dollars instead, she inserted the cash and pressed a couple buttons.

"Beep, boop, boop," she said.

"Come *on*, Judy," called Queen Victoria XXX, wobbling a little further down the street. Her hair was jutting out in all directions. She, the air around her, seemed to be glowing alongside the neon storefronts. There were either in future Los Angeles or ancient Tokyo.

"One friggin' *minute*!"

"JuuUUuudddyyy," sang the queen.

The machine clanged and hissed. A paper cup slid onto the tray.

"Come to mama," mumbled the scientist.

Coffee began sputtering out of the nozzle, then stopped, then turned into the clawed hand of a gremlin. The rest of the feral lizard-monster followed soon thereafter, chunks of machinery falling to the woman's feet as the creature pulled itself free.

"You're not coffee," said Judy, stumbling backward. She called up the street: "Hey, Vicky, this thing's not making coffee, it's making gramlins, d'you want a gramlin?"

***

"Yeah, gimme, like, three Long Island Iced Teas."

***

"I'll have two Scorpion Bowls, th'nk you."

***

"Nuclear Rainbow."

***

"Stormbringer, an' make it a double."

***

"What d'you mean yer outta whiskey?!"

***

Flames were rising from the collapsed frame of Tierney's Pub.

"Thish one's on me," said Judy Lin, raising a finger unsteadily into the air. "My bad."

***

The scientist climbed on top of the cloned president, her mouth all over his. She started pulling at the buttons on his shirt.

"Do it!" shouted Queen Victoria XXX from the passenger seat. "*DO IT!*"

Judy reached for her foot.

"Hey, where'sh my shoes?"

***

"What'd'ya mean yer outttta vokka?"

***

"GIVE ME ALL YOUR HOT DOGS!" roared the burly blonde man, hefting the hot dog cart over his head.

***

"Hey," barked the conductor, sliding open the door, "you can't be out here when the train's moving."

"Sorry," slurred Abraham Lincoln XVI, pressed up against the edge of the alcove at the back of the subway car, "eshtenu – eshtenuitting circumshtances."

"I don't give a crap. You two can't be between the cars when —"

Judy Lin, gripping the handle, pivoted sideways, aiming for the tracks, and hwarfed up, like, sixty percent of what she'd put away that evening. It took a while.

"Uh, yeah, OK," said the train operator, watching her go. "Just ... try not to die."

***

There was a ... dragon? Maybe?

But she was a good dragon and everybody ended up just playing cards together?

***

Thor Odinson and Queen Victoria XXX were standing around in their underwear in a laundromat. The clone was sitting on an idle dryer, while the thunder god was throwing clothes into a washing machine.

They both seemed very surprised by this.

"Where'd did everybody go?" asked Thor.

"Is this 'cause of the drinking or the time jumping?" asked the queen.

"More 'portantly," began the god, holding up his shirt, "who's brains is these?"

"It's whose," mumbled the clone. "W-H-O-S-E."

"What? How —"

"Yer not seeing the actual words you're speaking?"

"No."

The queen squinted, for a while.

"I probably shouldna drank that ayahuasca," she eventually mumbled. There was a loud, wet rumble from the general vicinity of her midsection. Her eyes went wide. "Oh no. Is ... Is there a bathroom in here?"

"I 've no idea," said the swaying pale-skinned man.

"Prob'ly not gonn' make it anyway," said the dark-skinned woman, lifting the lid of the dryer next to her. "Don't look." She added: "Or do. I'm not yer mom."

CHAPTER SEVENTEEN
TANGLED UP IN BLUE

SOMETIME THE NEXT SOMETHING, QUEEN VICTORIA XXX, THOR Odinson, and Jesus Christ woke up on the White House lawn.

"I feel ... like there's a joke here ..." mumbled the god.

"No. No talking," rasped the clone, clearly in the anguished throes of several different hangovers. Pulling herself into a sitting position, she looked down at her legs, then her arms and hands, and so on. She appeared to be wearing her faded black duster, over leather pants and a Kevlar-lined top. She had on a pair of reinforced, half-fingered gloves.

"What's ... This isn't what I was wearing last night. These are my hero clothes." Something like hope rose in her chest. "Did I change the past?"

"If you did, you didn't do a great job," said Thor, pointing toward the black hole tie-dyeing the horizon. "I think we just changed clothes." He turned his arm, stretched his legs, taking in one of a half dozen combinations of the only things he wore: boots, jeans, and a flannel shirt.

"Or maybe we had them changed for us?" he added, thinking causing more of a headache than usual. "I don't remember much after, like, the fourth bar we burned down."

"That's dumb," grumbled the queen. "You're dumb."

"I'm not the one who fucked me."

The clone stared at the god, squinted. Then, deflating: "I deserve that."

Beside them, Jesus Christ moaned indistinctly and rolled over onto his back. The world was spinning around him, and he had no idea if it was vertigo or if the world was actually spinning, faster and faster, endlessly, like a busted carousel.

"I'd like to get off now," he mumbled.

"That's what she said," said Thor.

"That is what I said," added Queen Victoria XXX.

The god's face fell. "Now *I* feel bad."

"You should."

"Hey," said Jesus, pointing, "what's that?"

Across the yard, a blurry shape approached them, gradually getting less and less blurry as it neared, and eventually revealing itself to be William H. Taft XLII. The big man knelt down next to the trio.

"I take it," said the Benevolent Dictator of FARTSSS, "that you were unsuccessful."

"Sorry," said the thunder god.

The cloned president shrugged.

"Hey, uh, Billy," began Queen Victoria XXX, head still swimming, "we saw Bo. Briefly. Didn't exactly get to talk much."

"Yeah? That's been happening," said William H. Taft XLII. Then: "How, uh, how was she doing?"

"She was doing really good, Billy," Thor gently answered.

"I got sassed by my younger self, too," added Queen Victoria XXX.

"Huh," said the president. "History seems to have its eyes on you."

"What?"

William H. Taft XLII stood up, his watch chain, the brass buttons on his military tunic catching the sunlight. He nodded his head toward the White House. "Something else showed up for you last night."

"OK ..." said the queen.

"Inside."

"OK."

"Where we should go? Now?"

"For real, Billy? Can't you just bring it out here?" she asked, leaning forward and rubbing her temples. "Moving seems like *a lot* right now."

"I mean, I *guess* so," mumbled William H. Taft XLII. "We had, like, a whole *thing* set up for you, but, sure, if you just want to shit all over –"

"It's fine, Billy," said a voice. A very familiar voice.

Queen Victoria XXX looked up, crippling migraine be damned.

Standing a short distance in front of her was Chester A. Arthur XVII. Reasonably tall and ruggedly handsome and heavily sideburned and in the flesh – his real, actual, original flesh. Not a cyborg, not a Frankenstein, not a hallucination or a hologram or a stuffed moose.

"Charlie?"

"Hey, Vicky."

The cloned queen stumbled to her feet and ran to him, throwing herself into his arms. The president grabbed her and swung her around.

"Charlie!"

"You know there's a giant black hole devouring the Earth, right?" he said, his gaze darting toward the giant black hole devouring the Earth. "Should we –"

"I don't care, baby," she said, tears in her eyes, his face in her hands.

"Then I don't either," said the president.

They started kissing, and they didn't stop for a good long while.

Meanwhile, twenty feet away ...

"Harsh," said Jesus Christ, struggling to sit up. "Weren't you two ... you know ..."

"Warm bodies on a cold night, buddy," answered the thunder god, smiling. He clapped his hand on his brother's back. "Come on, let's go find some coffee. You can tell me what you got up to after you left us last night."

"Oh, man, man," said the Middle Eastern man, stooped and unsteady on his feet, "you're not gonna believe it. As soon as I left the bar, like, *immediately*, I ran into Buddha and Shiva, and then we all piled into a cab and ..."

CHAPTER EIGHTEEN
NOW COMES THE PART OF OUR STORY THAT GETS A LITTLE BIT SAD

THE WORKSHOP – MORE LIKE A WAREHOUSE, REALLY – WAS uncharacteristically silent. Empty, too. Benches and tables were cluttered with equipment, with half-built conductors and motors, unfinished teleportational transponders and transmogrifiers and all kinds of other space-age shit.

But there was no one there doing anything with them.

William H. Taft XLII, a hemoglobic compressor engine in his arms, walked a few steps farther inside.

"Hello?" he called.

"Yeah," called a voice, low and sullen and from the shadows. "In the back, Billy."

Taking the engine with him, the cloned president walked the length of the warehouse, to the last workstation at the back. He found a man slumped forward, small and lean, covered in grease and scabs, his elbows on the table before him, his long hair falling forward.

"What's going on?" asked William H. Taft XLII, dropping the engine on a nearby bench. "What happened since you called?"

The man swiveled around on his stool. His eyes were red and dry.

"Why are we doing this, man?" asked Leonardo da Vinci XXIV.

"What do you mean, why? Because we have to."

"*This isn't going to work, Billy,*" roared the inventor, slamming his fist onto his workbench. "That's the hemoglobic compressor, right? The fucking *blood engine*? We're so far past science this is basically *witchcraft*. How fucked do we have to be that we've turned to God damned witchcraft?!"

"You know full well there's a –"

"Oh, for – Shove it out your ass, man!" shouted Leonardo da Vinci XXIV. "Even if we could get the – and I repeat – *blood engine* connected to the quantum core, which itself, by the way, still won't connect to the vacuum torpedo, which itself is already heavily reliant on ancient fucking *runes, it's not going to do shit*. We have no way of getting it airborne high enough and fast enough, and the singularity's too far gone anyway."

"Fuck you, Leo," snarled William H. Taft XLII, rage suddenly consuming him. He'd been through too much, seen too many of his friends die in his arms, to let things end this way, to watch anyone else he cared for be destroyed by a heartless and haphazard universe. He'd put too much of his own blood and sweat into rebuilding this world from dust and ash, chased away too many wives turning humanity into something actually worth saving.

And, by god – any of them, *all* of them – he'd save it again.

Through sheer force of will if he had to.

"We can fix this," said the president, his voice a cracking glacier.

"We can't, Billy," pleaded the small man. "We physically can't."

"Maybe you can't –" The big man shoved past the clone of the Italian painter. "– but I can. I can fix anything. I can fix *this*."

"You *can't*, man! Are you even fucking listening?! We – all of us – Archimedes and Albert and Grace and Franklin and fucking Marie – Marie! – we've tried literally everything and –"

"*I can fix this!*" he exploded. Then William H. Taft XLII grabbed the blood engine and hefted it onto da Vinci's workbench.

CHAPTER SEVENTEEN
TILL YOU ALL JUST DISAPPEAR

THE SKY HAD BEEN VARYING SHADES OF DARK PURPLE FOR A WHILE now, save for the parts that were black and blue and dematerializing. Only with tremendous difficulty was Chester A. Arthur XVII, reloaded from an earlier save point and currently sitting on the roof of the Rainbow House, able to discern where the sun was supposed to be.

He was, as far as he could tell, watching it set for the last time.

"Fuck."

There was a knock on the skylight next to him. He turned, found Queen Victoria XXX climbing onto the roof.

"How you doing?" she asked, settling in beside him. "Come to terms with oblivion yet?"

"Getting there," said Chester A. Arthur XVII. "The sky's pretty, though."

"In that 'science can't explain how it hasn't killed us all yet' kind of way, sure."

He smiled. "What other definition of 'pretty' is there?"

"Come on," she said, taking his hand. "Inside." Her eyes flashed. "We've still got a few hours and I'm damn sure gonna make 'em count."

CHAPTER EIGHTEEN
IF I HAD A HAMMER

THE FORTY-SECOND CLONE OF AMERICA'S TWENTY-SEVENTH president was hunched over the worktable, sweating through his undershirt; his hands, his arms, a blur of activity. He measured this and mathed that, punching numbers into a tablet, into his phone, scratching down others on scrap paper. He pulled out lengths of wire, clamps and couplings, screws and bolts, ransacking the other stations. The big man drilled and welded, and, when that didn't work, shoved things together, cramming gears and outlets into one another through brute force.

"Billy," said Catherine the Great XLIX.

"Leo send you in here?" he replied, not looking up.

"He's worried about you," she said. "*I'm* worried about you."

"That seems like a gross misuse of your time."

"You're talking like there's any left."

"Where's Artemis?" asked the president, and not gently.

"Trying to do what you're doing," the cloned empress explained, "the *impossible*. She thinks she can move the moon."

"Maybe she can."

"Probably. Won't do any good, though. Not now."

"So you left her?" William H. Taft XLII put down his tools, turned his head.

"She turned into an eighty-foot-tall ethereal being and started walking on the air," said Catherine the Great LXIX. "Wasn't a whole lot I could do after that."

"I'm ... I'm sorry," he said, slouching forward. The benevolent dictator breathed deeply, his shoulders rising and falling. He swiveled toward the other clone for a moment, then abruptly returned to the workbench.

"But either help me or get out," he growled.

CHAPTER EIGHTEEN
STARS YOU NEVER COULD SEE

PARKER PETERSEN AND MARY ANNE HOLMES HAD, LIKE SO MANY others, felt a need to actually *see* the supermassive extradimensional black hole that would soon be killing them. After all, they'd made it through the panicking, and the rioting, and the ugly-crying until they were dehydrated. They'd thought long and talked hard and resigned themselves to Earth's impending erasure from existence.

The least the universe could do now was make it worth their while.

The universe, for its part, seemed to agree.

Microwaving some popcorn and unbarricading the door, Parker and Mary Anne were greeted by a sight to end all sights – literally. Taking up most of the western sky, the pitch black singularity, the empty heart of the black hole, was ringed by swirling, admiral blue tendrils of interdimensional radiation, crackling and effervescent like a neon sign, a kaleidoscope of stars caught in their wake. Add in some reds and oranges from the occasional floating city paying the price for its hubris, and the imminent end of everything may as well have been a van Gogh painting, albeit from his oft-forgotten Doomsayer Period.

Sitting down on the rickety wooden steps of Parker's apartment, barefoot and cold, the two twentysomethings were struck appropriately dumb by the magnificence of nature, frozen by the awesomeness of science barreling down on them, their mouths open, popcorn not quite there. Facing, for the first time and absolutely without question, the vastness of the universe and their own paltry insignificance, the couple couldn't help but feel something stir within their very souls.

And then, after that got boring, their pants.

Letting the popcorn fall and spill across the sidewalk, Mary Anne and Parker hurled their bodies together, his hands in her hair, her hands on his thighs, their mouths never separating. Fueled by adrenaline and abandon and still-being-in-their-twenties, this particular encounter was shaping up to be something special.

This, after all, was no mere hook-up, no last gasp Hail Mary. No, this, though neither of them was *entirely* sure about it yet, was true love.

Which is precisely why what happened next, happened next.

With a brilliant flash and the horrendous crashing sound of physics breaking in half, a flying saucer – shiny silver and lined with blinking lights, on the smaller side as far as these things went – appeared over the street before the young lovers, hovering twenty feet above the pavement.

"Whaaat the hell," inquired Mary Anne, looking at the ship.

Within a matter of moments, the air directly in front of the couple fizzled and popped, then settled down again in the shape of two aliens. They were short and green, with heads like upside-down scrotums. Their species didn't appear to have discovered clothes yet.

"Yo," said the first one, holding something that looked like a mobile phone up to something that looked like its throat.

"You guys want to live or what?" asked the second, doing the same.

"Whaaat ..." parroted Parker.

"Do. You. Want. To. *Live*." The alien removed the translation contraption and grumbled something unintelligible – though obviously insulting – to its partner.

"What my friend here is *trying* to say," said the first alien, "is that we're a little pressed for time, yeah? I mean, you guys are aware of the scientifically-impossible singularity gobbling up your atmosphere, right?"

"We are," replied Parker.

"That, somehow, is the only part of this that makes any sense," added Mary Anne.

"OK, good. Then let's start there: You're planet is screwed. *Screeewwwed*. As such, someone sent out a distress beacon. We found it, and now we're here to rescue you. And by you, we mean *you two*, specifically."

"I'm confused," said Parker.

"Yeah, no shit," said the second alien. "Thankfully we're not here for your brains."

"Q'en, come on," said the first one. Then, turning back to the humans: "OK, let's try this again. I'm Fr'r and this is my partner Q'en. We're from the planet ... Well, it doesn't have a great translation into any Earth consonants, but, for the sake of argument, you can call it F't Blottogr'ls. Our planet — and, again, this isn't a direct equivalence — is powered by love. Pure, untarnished love."

"*Powered* by?" asked Parker.

"Like batteries?" asked Mary Anne.

"Yes ..." Fr'r hesitantly agreed, "but not like you're thinking. You're not plugged into anything or shoved inside of something."

"We're nowhere near as primitive as your outdated human prisons," added Q'en.

"So, then, what?" asked the young human male. "Like, zoos?"

"And you siphon off our ... *feelings*?" asked the human female.

"More like a wilderness preserve," said Fr'r, raising its knee, the F't Blottogr'lian equivalent of a shrug. "Lot of room."

"Huh."

"It's not as bad as you're making it sound, I promise."

"Besides ..." Q'en tossed a thumb-like appendage towards the swirling vortex of annihilation over its shoulder.

"That is an excellent point," said Parker, getting up from the stairs. "You in?" he asked his girlfriend, holding out a hand.

"Are you kidding me?" said Mary Anne, taking it and pulling herself up. "I worked *retail*. Let's get the hell off this craphole planet."

"That's the spirit," said Q'en.

"Great," added Fr'r. "Now let's get going. We've still got, like, a hundred more couples to collect and the clock is ticking."

"Only a hundred?" asked Parker.

The aliens cocked what passed for their eyebrows.

"No, right," said the young man, "my bad. Heard it as soon as I said it."

"Honestly," said the second alien, "it is just like Earth to kill itself and destroy the *entire fucking galaxy* along the way."

CHAPTER SEVENTEEN
DREAM TO ME

"CAN'T SLEEP?" ASKED JESUS CHRIST, ON HIS BACK, HIS HANDS behind his head.

"No."

"Worried about the end of the world?"

"Yes," said Mary Magdalene, rolling closer and laying her head on his chest. "Is it too late to start praying for a miracle?"

"Can't hurt," he said.

CHAPTER EIGHTEEN
JUST FOR ONE DAY

AN ENORMOUS, RATTLETRAP WINNEBAGO MATERIALIZED OUT OF seemingly nowhere. After a moment, and with unnecessary force, the door was thrown open, clattering against the side of the motor home. A woman in a tweed sport jacket leaned out, one hand still gripping the interior handle. Another woman in a hoodie leaned out behind her.

"Right," said the first woman, "we need to —"

"Where's the ground?"

"What?"

"The ground," said the second woman, looking down at the absolute nothing on which the vehicle was perched. "Where the hell is it?"

"Benedict Cumberbatch."

Carissa Gonzalez-Patel ducked back inside, rushing to the rear of the cluttered RV and frantically inspecting the cobbled-together time-teleporter that took up most of the bedroom. She hurried from connection to connection, reactor to reactor, lifting this and sliding that and, in a moment of deep thought, leaning her palm against one of the overworked processing towers.

"Ow, fuck," she groaned, pulling her hand away. Then, eyes darting across the machinery, she called to the front: "What are our planetary coordinates?"

Her wife, Amber, grabbed the control tablet from the stained Formica counter and tapped it a few times.

"We, uh, we don't have any," she said, violently poking the screen some more.

"You're sure you're reading that right, right?"

"Yes!" Amber shouted. "I have a Ph.D. too!"

"I know, but it took you seven years, and it was in art history."

"Let it go, lady!"

"I don't get it," said Carissa, brow knitted like a wool hat, making her way toward the front of the motor home. "Why are we in space? We're supposed to be in the Consolidated Phukital parking lot, six hours before their asinine plan to set off a hydrogen bomb and kill us all."

"Did you forget to adjust for the Earth's position in space when you made the jump?" asked Amber, somewhere between gently and condescendingly. "Its orbit and rotation?"

"Of course I adjusted for those," replied her wife with a sneer.

"Then why, my love, my sweetheart, are we *already inside of the black hole we came here to stop?!*" shouted Amber, hurling the tablet through the doorway and into the endless void surrounding the Winnebago. "We're basically sitting on the event horizon!"

"I don't know, *honey*," snarled Carissa. "I don't know why we're – Oh, wait, wait. I do. I know what happened."

"You didn't account for the black hole, did you? The increased gravity, the strange effects it has on time?"

"I did not."

"God damn it, Carissa," groaned the other woman, slumping onto the tattered couch.

"That's kind of an overreaction, isn't it, babe?" said the woman in the blazer, placing a hand on Amber's shoulder and squeezing gently. "We're in a time-teleporter. We'll just, you know ..." She hopped in place.

"We can't do that, you dumb dummy," growled her wife, shoving the other woman's tweed-covered arm away. "For one thing, I just threw the control tablet into outer space, and, for another, it takes, like, thirty minutes to reprogram the destinations and get everything running, and that's after a mandatory thirty-minute cooldown."

"And we don't –"

"No, not even close."

"Huh." Carissa scrunched up her face, sat down on the sofa beside Amber. The windows behind them were black as pitch. "Guess we really fucked this one up then."

"*You.* You fucked this one up," corrected Amber, leaning her head back, her eyes closed.

"Well, *whoever* may or may not have been at fault here, let me ... Let me just say thank you, Amber, for being my companion on this –"

"I am *your wife*, lady," roared the woman in the hoodie, springing back to life. "Don't come at me with this companion shit like I'm some kind of sidekick." Amber gasped, like a put-upon assistant on a British sitcom. "Or *a dog*?! Do you think of me like I'm your *pet*?!"

"Not ... *all* the time ..."

"You *unbelievable* bitch!"

"You're the one that's always saying Cleo's an equal part of the family!"

"Because she is!"

"She's a *Shih-Tzu!*" Carissa snapped. "And if she's so equal, why is it such an insult if I referred to *you* as a dog?"

"So you were!"

"I said '*if*!'"

"Oh my God!" shouted Amber, rising angrily and stomping in front of Carissa. "You know what, babe? That's it. This is the last friggin' time! Why don't you," she began slowly, calmer than she'd been expecting, "go fu–"

The Winnebago disappeared into the black hole – although, to any outside observers, it merely stretched infinitely, a streak of beige and burgundy slowly thinning and dissipating into nothing.

In a sense, they never actually died.

Amber Gonzalez-Patel simply screamed at her wife forever.

CHAPTER EIGHTEEN
DRINKING WHISKEY AND RYE

SOMETHING THAT SORT OF LOOKED LIKE SOMETHING THAT MIGHT actually do something was beginning to take shape on the workbench. William H. Taft XLII, drenched and dirty, grabbed a small sledgehammer, began slamming it against a metal plug.

Outside the warehouse, the wind was picking up, the windows rattling. The lights above the table flickered.

The big man continued hammering, methodical and determined.

The wind began to howl, like a werewolf after being stood up. The building began to rock, like a teenage band without any self-awareness or ability, in a bar without a stage or any patrons. Things began to topple off tables, like a drunken pole dancer.

But the clone kept hammering, the clanging tattoo ringing out faster and faster. Then, more and more frantic, uneven. Before the big man finally just screamed and started throwing tools everywhere.

"Fuck!"

Lifting the blood engine over his head, he hurled the compressor to the floor, then kicked it so hard it dented, slid, and slammed into another workbench.

"*FUCK!*"

William H. Taft XLII fell to his knees.

"I can fix this," he whimpered. "I can fix anything."

"Not this, man," said Leonardo da Vinci XXIV, eyes red and wet, "I'm sorry." He put a hand on the other man's shoulder. "Come on. Everyone else is in the lounge."

CHAPTER SEVENTEEN
JUDGEMENT DAY

AMEN-RA, EGYPTIAN GOD-KING OF THE SUN AND CREATOR OF THE universe, was watching television. A *Wheel of Fortune* rerun, specifically.

"The Fast and the Furious," he mumbled. "The solution is very clearly —"

The screen turned black. The power went out.

With tremendous effort, Amen-Ra removed himself from his armchair and, tying his bathrobe tight around his waist, shuffled over to the window. He pulled up the blinds.

The world – his world – was coming apart at the seams. The planet he'd so meticulously built, from the burning core to the abundant wildlife to the thinning air, was being ripped apart and turned to nothing before his very eyes.

He shrugged. "Maybe next time."

CHAPTER EIGHTEEN
NO ONE SINGS LIKE YOU ANYMORE

ERIN MCCAFFERTY AND JORGE REYES, HANDS CLASPED AND hearts heavy, sat on their couch, wide eyes on the widescreen across from them. The local news – cycling through every anchor and set the station had had over the past twenty years – was airing clips of the world's tallest cities being warped and smudged and erased, like someone learning how to use Photoshop for the first time. The floating cities were already gone, said the newswoman, and, obviously, the mid-size buildings were next, followed by the regular ones. Citizens were advised to try to find a basement, or a gutter, or a fallout shelter, and press themselves flat against the floor.

This wouldn't actually do much, however, explained the newsman, given how utterly and completely fu–

Erin turned off the television, tossing the remote onto the coffee table. She pulled her husband's arm tight, nestling her greying head into his chest. Jorge laid his head on hers. Around them, their walls flickered and fell and reappeared, clean and brand new, like when they'd first purchased the house half a lifetime ago.

"We had a good run," she said.

"We did," he replied, kissing the top of her head.

"I'm glad it was you."

Jorge Reyes pulled Erin McCafferty closer, holding her tightly.

He never let her go again.

CHAPTER TWENTY
THE END, FOREVER

THOR ODINSON, THE NORSE GOD OF THUNDER; QUEEN VICTORIA XXX, the last extant clone of the last ruler of the House of Hanover; and a time-displaced Chester A. Arthur XVII sat on the elaborately manicured Rainbow House lawn, watching as New New York, D.C. was sucked away into the ravenous maw of the extradimensional black hole bearing down on them.

Red, white, and blue federal buildings twisted and unraveled, the color draining out of them along the way. Slate and chrome and glass shattered and spun and stretched, like funhouse mirrors reflecting a quarry caught up in a tornado.

The horizon – or what passed for it – was yanked upward in the middle, like the mouth of a fish on a hook.

Everything else was black, utter and complete. The black hole was so close and so wide, no one could see the edges, the spinning blue tentacles of otherdimensional energy surging and grabbing.

And the wind, full of sound and fury, howling, carrying screams and cries and rending metal, signifying the all-encroaching nothing devouring everything.

It was only a matter of minutes now.

"I guess this is goodbye," said Thor, raising his voice above the din. He held up a half-drunk bottle of champagne. The clones did the same.

"For Bo," he said.

"For Ali," said Chester A. Arthur XVII.

"For Billy," said the queen, "wherever he is."

"For Mark and Timmy."

"For Jesus and Artemis and Cathy."

"For Sheila," said Thor.

"For Charlie," said Queen Victoria XXX, crashing her bottle into the others.

"For Catrina," said the thunder god.

Guzzling the last of the alcohol – the very last on Earth – the trio braced for impact, clenching their butts, hands digging into the soil, wondering how it would feel to be torn apart atom by atom.

Not great, they assumed.

They closed their eyes, scrunched up their faces, their shoulders.

They breathed deep, held that breath like it was their last.

Then a horse neighed, louder than the rushing air, than the destruction around them.

Cautiously, the three opened their eyes.

A massive woman on a winged, white mare was standing in front of them.

"What the actual fuck," said Queen Victoria XXX.

"Brünnhilde?" asked the thunder god.

"'tis time to come home, Thor," said the Valkyrie.

"Like, *home* home?" he asked. "Valhalla's back? Asgard? All of it?"

"Verily," said the shieldmaiden. "When thou reached thine true potential here on Midgard, thou didst prove all of the mortal science wrong. Thou reinstated all of the religions, and all of the heavens." She pulled an enormous, gleaming sword from her back. "But, come, time is fleeting."

The Valkyrie slashed her blade through the air, a couple times, each cut severing reality itself. A rectangular patch of existence fell away, dissipating into nothing. In its place, a brightly glowing portal, and on the other side ...

"What are we looking at?" asked Queen Victoria XXX.

"That's Valhalla," said Thor, staggering to his feet, "the hall in which the souls of heroes slain in battle are received by Odin."

"Thou didst put up a good fight," said Brünnhilde.

Two figures stepped into the light. As their eyes adjusted, the earthbound trio could see Catrina Dalisay and Ali Şahin standing on the other side of the gateway.

"Hey, buddy," said Catrina, a smile taking up most of her face. The small woman looked less gossamer than the last time Thor had seen her, though still not quite real. She seemed to be glowing with an indissoluble joy. And, judging by her flowing robes, it looked like she'd finally been allowed to change out of her laundry day sweatpants.

"Catrina ..." said the thunder god.

Behind him, the color began draining from the Rainbow House, flecks of paint and loose bricks and a couple of the weaker columns sailing through the air.

"Might wanna get a move on there," said the dead woman.

"Oh, right," he said, rushing toward the portal.

One foot in the gateway, Thor stopped and turned around.

Queen Victoria XXX and Chester A. Arthur XVII were still sitting on the ground.

The thunder god furrowed his brow, then extended his hand.

"You coming?" he asked.

The Valkyrie lowered her sword in front of the Norseman.

"They cannot pass," she said.

"Are you fucking serious, Hildy?" roared the burly god. The sky – or what was left of it – began crackling with lightning. "You know I outrank you, right?"

"Thor," said Queen Victoria XXX, standing now, her hands around his. "It's OK."

"We're homunculi, remember?" said Chester A. Arthur XVII, shrugging slightly from where he remained sitting. "No souls."

"Oh. Oh, right," said the crestfallen blonde man. "That's a fucking bummer."

"You're telling me," said the queen.

"So ... What are you gonna do?"

Queen Victoria XXX shrugged, looked around. "Watch it all come tumbling down, I guess."

And then – as Thor and Brünnhilde disappeared into Valhalla, as reality repaired itself just in time to get torn apart again – they did.

EPILOGUE
DEUS EX SPACE INVADER

THE QUEEN AND THE PRESIDENT STOOD HAND-IN-HAND AS EVERYTHING around them ended.

But they weren't worried.

They didn't cry.

They were together.

Which is precisely why what happened next, happened next.

With a horrendous crashing sound, barely perceptible over the cacophony of reality being sucked away, a flying saucer materialized above them. The door opened and a tiny green man with a head like a ballsack appeared in the entryway.

"Hey," he shouted, "you guys Chester A. Arthur XVII and Queen Victoria XXX? We're here to rescue you."

ACKNOWLEDGEMENTS

Thanks for reading the *Exponential Apocalypse* books. They're done now. That's nine-hundred-and-thirty-one or so pages you can't unread.

In memoriam, here's a comprehensive list of everyone and everything that is responsible, in some fashion, for those pages, whether it was because they helped me or inspired me or because I shamelessly ripped them off at some point, be it consciously or otherwise.

Please note, this list also, conveniently, doubles as a list of things I wholeheartedly endorse and/or recommend, assuming you were looking for that information.

Now, without further ado, my heartfeltiest thank yous to: adverbs; Ally Malinenko, ancient religions of all kinds; *Army of Darkness* (and the *Evil Dead* franchise generally); assorted classic rock bands not mentioned by name below; Batman (but, like, the *idea* of him, not any particular iteration, except for maybe *The Animated Series* version); Benedict Cumberbatch; Blake's green chile cheeseburgers; *Bloody, Bloody Andrew Jackson*; *Bob's Burgers*; *Broad City*; Bruce Springsteen; Chris Cornell and Soundgarden; *Clone High* probably, in hindsight; *Cracked*; *Community*; Danger Slater; Dolores O'Riordan and the Cranberries; dinosaurs; Douglas Adams; *Dragonball Z*; *Futurama*; *Hamilton*; history; Jamaican ginger ale; *Jurassic Park* (but only the book and the first movie); Kurt Vonnegut; Mike, Sam, and Laura at *Jersey Devil Press*; my family; my former job; my former professors; old Marvel comics (and the new ones, why not); old movies; *People of Earth* and/or *This Island Earth* and/or *Mystery Science Theater 3000*; *Pinky and the Brain*; Prince; Pringles' salt and vinegar chips; REO Speedwagon; Stanford Hospital and everyone who works there; *Star Wars*; Steve and Sarita; *The Simpsons*, probably; Tom Petty, and the Heartbreakers; Uncle Paul; werewolves and the requisite lore; Warren Zevon; William Shakespeare; and everyone that's purchased an *Exponential Apocalypse* book in the past, everyone that's reviewed or recommended one, and everyone else that wants to be thanked.

Also, a special – and long overdue – shout out to my Uncle Mike, who gave me the first three books of the *Hitchhiker's Guide to the Galaxy* series during my first hospitalization when I was fifteen. As cheesy and cliché as it may sound, those books changed my life and are directly responsible for the *Exponential Apocalypse* books, as well as, like, everything else I've written.

And laster, but certainly not leaster, my wife Monica. Thank you for being everything to me, and for putting up with my shit, both metaphorically and literally. (Cystic fibrosis is not kind to the digestive system, guys.)

And, finally, a quick note to our dogs, Brock and Harvey: It's adorable when you sit on my lap and put your paws on the keyboard, or your head on my hand, but, honestly, that makes it impossible to type and you failed to contribute *anything* of value to this or any book.

Thanks for absolutely nothing, puppies.

ABOUT THE AUTHOR

Eirik Gumeny is the author of the *Exponential Apocalypse* series, the latest – and last! – of which you've just read. Congratulations! His short fiction can be found all over the internet and in various anthologies, and he has contributed to *Cracked* and *The New York Times*. He is an avid fan of both Shakespeare and fart jokes.

Eirik was born with cystic fibrosis and was kind of disgusting to be around for a while. In 2014, he received a double lung transplant and may have briefly died. He got better.

Born in the suburban sprawl of northeastern New Jersey, he currently lives in Albuquerque, New Mexico, where he regularly has to fight giant atomic ants with a flamethrower.

Website: www.egumeny.com
Twitter: @egumeny
Facebook: egumeny

ALSO BY THE AUTHOR

ENDNOTES

---

[i] Legendary creatures from the Middle Ages that used poop as a weapon. See Pliny the Elder's *Naturalis Historia* for more information. Or this author's *Revenge-aroni*.

[ii] Quetzalcoatl destroyed most of Mexico and all of Central America a few years before the events of the first *Exponential Apocalypse*. Canada, meanwhile, lost half of its northern holdings during the solar wave-induced Great Melt of '36, an event that was not mentioned in any of this author's books until now. Lucky you!

[iii] After the Gorilla Liberation Front hijacked an orbital laser, they decimated human society and ended the world for the sixteenth time, turning Washington, D.C. into a series of forever-smoldering piles of rubble. Later, during the events of *Dead Presidents*, the ruined remnants were wrecked even more, this time by Andrew Jackson II and Nikola Tesla's earthquake machine.

[iv] Though known primarily for their copy machines, the Xerox Corporation is actually crazy involved in all kinds of digital document solutions, commercial printing, and, more importantly — especially for the purposes of this narrative — has a longstanding research partnership with Stanford University. Together — along with several other investors, including Samsung and NEC — they created PARC, a massive R&D company/facility in Palo Alto. There, Xerox researches clean energy, metamaterials, and "sensemaking," wherein technology and cognitive understanding are brought together. All of this, by the way, is completely true, meaning that the Xerox Corporation creating human clones is probably the least fantastical idea in any of the *Exponential Apocalypse* books thus far.

[v] After being cloned, the Abraham Lincolns — like all the rest of the cloned politicians — were forced to fight themselves to the death, the winner being allowed to go free. Unlike all the rest of the cloned politicians, *five* Lincolns walked out of that deathmatch, choosing teamwork over vivisection. Together, they worked as a force for good for years — often alongside William H. Taft XLII — right up until three of them were killed mercilessly during the Las Vegas Massacre. The two remaining presidents, Abraham Lincoln LVI and Abraham Lincoln XVI, split up shortly thereafter, grieving and angry, unable to look at one another. Abraham Lincoln LVI dropped off the grid entirely, while Abraham Lincoln XVI returned to his only two true loves: serving drinks and getting in fights.

www.ingramcontent.com/pod-product-compliance
Lightning Source LLC
Chambersburg PA
CBHW030552130626
46552CB00006B/2521